After All
Murphy Brother Stories, book 7
Jennifer Rodewald

ROOTED PUBLISHING

After All

ISBN: 978-1-7347421-8-3

Cover design by Evelyne Labelle at Carpe Librum Book Design
www.carpelibrumbookdesign.com

First printing edition 2021.

Rooted Publishing

McCook, NE 69001

Email: jen@authorjenrodewald.com

https://authorjenrodewald.com/

AFTER ALL

ISBN: 978-1-7347421-8-3

Any references to events, real people, or real places are used
fictitiously. Names, characters, and places are products of the author's
imagination, and any similarities to real events are purely accidental.

Front-cover image from Shutterstock Images and Lightstock photos,
used with licensed permission. Design by Jennifer Rodewald.

First printing edition 2021.

Rooted Publishing

McCook, NE 69001

Email: jen@authorjenrodewald.com

https://authorjenrodewald.com/

Contents

"If we confess our sins, he is faithful and just and will forgive us our sins and purify us from all unrighteousness."

First John 1:9

Chapter One

(IN WHICH THERE IS REALITY)

He'd gone too far.

Brayden had known that uncomfortable fact for much longer than he'd been willing to admit. Even now, admitting the annoying reality wasn't exactly done with a submissive attitude. He'd much rather continue to do what he wanted to do—ignore his Christian upbringing and the conscience that had been honed to biblical values since childhood. It suited real life better. At least, if one wanted to have a life.

Brayden Murphy most certainly wanted a life. After all, every one of his six brothers had landed on happy living, no sweat. Why shouldn't he?

Well, that was sort of true. There had been a few hiccups in his blessed brothers' lives. Tyler's accident being the most glaring example. But hey, look at him now. Living the dreamy life of a sponsored athlete and getting back the girl he'd always loved. So, happy after all—and with a baby on the way as the cherry on top.

How about that?

There was also Matt, with his always-ready-with-something-positive-to-say wife and their three angelic girls. And Jacob! The confirmed snob of the older half of siblings, come 'round to good graces within the fold, and living pretty well off his talented wife's writing while they raised up a son who looked just like him. How about Jackson? The prankster who often didn't know when to quit, now making his living by telling audiences about his idiotic stunts, making them laugh, then coming home to a wife who hadn't even loved him at the beginning of their marriage. Mackenzie clearly adored Jackson now, as they both adored their daughter and son and anticipated another little one soon. And Connor? That perfect older brother lived tucked away at an idyllic lake resort with his beloved wife and son.

That brought him to the closest brother Brayden had in age—Brandon. Brandon the bold. Brandon the stern-faced boy. Brandon the unforgiving.

Brandon the ridiculously smitten newlywed. How did a guy agree to an arranged marriage only to loathe that intended fiancée at the start, and still come out on the right side of love?

All of them had. Every one of his older brothers had been lucky in love and were living the dream.

That had not been Brayden's story. The love of his life, the girl he'd planned to be with forever since he'd been fifteen years old, up and got married a year before. To some guy in uniform she'd known for like five seconds. Yeah, he was still bitter about it, and wasn't sorry for that. He had every right to be angry. But he wasn't going to let Leah's betrayal end his pursuit of happiness.

Brayden had to fight for his happy. And he did, every way he could.

But.

He'd gone too far, and right then and there he couldn't shush that truth no matter how much he'd prefer to have it silenced.

That Sunday, which happened to be Easter Sunday, Brayden found himself planted in church for the first time in months, sandwiched between his father and his older brother Jackson. All the worse for it, too, because the sensation of utter failure had been hard enough to ignore as the congregation celebrated the resurrection of Jesus Christ. The sinner's path to redemption. If that sinner chose to walk it.

Why did church always have to feel so . . . so . . . judgmental? Made him feel like a slimy good-for-nothing scoundrel of a man. But he wasn't that bad, surely. After all, he wasn't really hurting anyone. Two consenting adults . . .

Audrey *was* an adult. Legally, she was, anyway, and old enough to know her own mind. Still, he hadn't meant to let things get so out of hand. It was just that she was all young adoration and sweet passion. Everything Leah had been back when she was his. Audrey's easy fit into his arms had soothed the raw burns in his heart when he was with her. And the best part was, she thought he was a man who lived up to his Murphy name.

Actually, that last part was bittersweet, for a couple of reasons. Leah had known exactly who Brayden was . . . and wasn't. Might be the reason she'd chosen someone else. Having Audrey think otherwise was way more comfortable, until Brayden dwelled on the fact she was measuring him against the Murphy brother she knew and probably had crushed on first.

Brandon.

Brandon, the image of their perfect father, in face, form, and action. The brother who would forever cast a shadow in which Brayden had been appointed to walk.

But Brayden willfully ignored that part of their relationship where Audrey believed he would live up to the standards Brandon had cast. Why complicate things? Audrey was his easy happy right now. That was enough.

Shifting uncomfortably in his chair, Brayden cast a quick glance around the sanctuary. If the people lining the chairs knew how he did everyday life—specifically on the weekends—since he'd left Sugar Pine, they'd tell him he was on the highway to hell. Wild parties. Excessive drinking. And last weekend with Audrey . . . Keen discomfort pulled a tight knot in his middle. Right after they expressed utter shock—*a Murphy boy! How could that happen?*—they'd shove him out the door, and good riddance to him for choosing such a life.

Then there would be his own family.

Dad would likely be the first one to show him the door. Which, truthfully, would sting pretty good—the very reason Brayden had kept the details of his life to himself, and had done so for quite a while.

Most days Brayden didn't care what others thought. A bold proclamation he'd spat out to stern-faced Brandon on more than one occasion. Mostly it was true, because he refused to think about the opinions of anyone else. His life, his choices. When such nagging ideas that he might be disappointing someone intruded upon his life of self-gratification, Brayden swatted them away with a slug (or five) of JB and the echoing mantra that had been his long-held justification: everyone else gets what they want. Why shouldn't he take his?

Why shouldn't I? His steamed thoughts rolled heavenward. Fitting, since he was in church. *Seems like You ran out of favors. All I ever asked for was Leah . . .*

Was it sacrilege to pick a fight with God in the middle of an Easter service?

Did he care?

The pit of his stomach churned, and Brayden rolled both fists as he tucked them under his arms.

"You okay, son?" Dad leaned just close enough to whisper.

Brayden grunted a "yup."

Dad placed a solid, work-chapped hand on Brayden's shoulder and squeezed. "It's good to have you here again."

The lava in Brayden's gut bubbled and rolled, and he resented the guilt Dad triggered. Did his father do it on purpose? Maybe.

Maybe Brandon had told their dad about Brayden's un-Murphy-like living. He'd certainly spent enough time telling Brayden what he thought of his choices.

She's young, Brayden. Don't go screwing up her life because Leah disappointed you.

She's innocent, Brayden. And she certainly looks at you like there's a future between you two. Don't do to her what Leah did to you. It isn't right.

Brandon the bold. Always insisting he knew the right way to go. Always frowning on anyone who didn't see things his way. As if he could understand. Clearly he didn't. For example, saying that Leah disappointed Brayden? Might as well call the Pacific a puddle. *Disappointed* didn't even come close to what Brayden felt when it came to Leah Thedford. *Watson* now. She'd been Brayden's first love. His first kiss. First promise. First . . . *everything*. She was supposed to be his last—and he hers. They'd sworn it to each other. There wasn't a word for that—certainly not *disappointed*.

And as for the way Audrey looked at him . . .

Balderdash.

Audrey was with Brayden because Brandon wasn't available—he'd married her best friend. Brayden wasn't her first choice. Recalling the gooey expression Audrey wore—and likely didn't even realize it—when Brandon filled her view moments before Brayden first met her—told him all. *Smitten girl* had been the broadcast of that look, no mistake about it. Brayden was the stand-in who looked close enough to pretend. That was all.

Anyway, it wasn't anyone else's business. Not Dad's. Certainly not Brandon's.

Audrey Smith stared at the counter in the bathroom she and Megan had shared until Megan had become Mrs. Murphy. A lump bulged in her throat, hot tears blurring her vision.

This was *not* good.

All her life she'd been the pride and joy of her parents. The little Smith family had enjoyed an easy closeness that seemed rare when Audrey had surveyed her schoolmates. Largely, their closeness had come because she was Mom and Dad's sweet girl. Their good girl. Their smart girl. Their only child, and a quiet, compliant one at that. She'd worked beside them, making meals, cleaning rooms, doing dishes, weeding flower beds. And most recently, working on rebuilding the small home that had been lost to a fire the summer before. A project that gained massive contribution from the Murphy family, as all the boys knew construction quite well. Brandon had rallied his dad and brothers, and they'd shown up often.

Audrey had particularly enjoyed that. One brother was still single, and despite Brandon and Megan's warnings, Brayden hadn't lost interest.

A sob lurched through Audrey's chest. She'd always been a good girl. *Always.* How could she have let this happen?

She was three weeks from graduating from high school. There would be a party, and Mom would cry. Dad might too. Megan would gush about how proud she was of Audrey. And Mr. and Mrs. Alexander would no doubt be very generous to her, as they always had been to all three Smiths, telling her that she was their bonus daughter. Not empty words, as their actions proved their hearts.

All their pride and enthusiasm and excitement would eventually fall to pieces. One large crash, and everything would shatter. She'd lose their respect.

Blinking back tears, Audrey's vision cleared long enough to see two pink lines in the tiny view pane of the stick.

Two pink lines let her know everything was about to splinter.

She would disappoint everyone.

Including Brayden. He wasn't ready for this. Truth be told, Audrey had come to a stifling realization that when it came to her, to them, Brayden's heart hadn't gone where hers had. She was his rebound—the distraction he'd chosen to stave off the ache in his heart left by the girl he'd intended to spend forever with. He'd not gotten over Leah, not in the year since she'd married someone else, and certainly not in Audrey's arms.

As that man surfaced in her mind, her heart clenched. She'd been warned about him—that he was wild and not who he should be. That his heart had been broken and bitterness had spilled out. Audrey hadn't cared. Brayden had been the first guy ever who hadn't gone for Megan first. His attention had skimmed over her friend-rival and gone straight to Audrey, and that had done it. She'd drunk in the way those rich brown eyes consumed her, and everything from that moment had been a slippery slope.

And there she was, at the bottom of the muddy hill. In the mire of choices that have consequences. The most agonizing part of it was that she had no idea what Brayden would do. Because the reality was, though he was Brandon Murphy's brother, Brayden was nothing like the steady, somewhat stern, but extraordinarily good man who had married Megan last fall. In fact, Brayden was Brandon's opposite in nearly every way.

The final, crushing blow was the truth Audrey had realized too late: Brayden didn't love her, and he wasn't likely to start. She was the stand-in for Leah, and nothing more. The willing distraction Brayden had used to numb the sting of Leah's rejection.

Tears rolled down her hot cheeks freely as her heart wrenched. Now it wasn't simply a broken heart. No, it was so much bigger. Worse.

Now . . . now she was pregnant. And entirely alone.

Chapter Two

(IN WHICH SECRETS LOOM LARGE)

Brayden tossed a tennis ball at the wall across from his bed, mindlessly catching it off the bounce as it returned. Though he stared hard, he saw nothing as his thoughts turned over what to do. The weekend was coming, which should be a relief, as classes were demanding this second semester of medical school. Seemed like all the studying for disease and therapeutics, clinical skills, and the upcoming step 1 board exam should have been plenty to keep his mind occupied. Especially since finals were looming in a week, and then he'd only have five weeks to finish prepping for that first board exam, his future in medical school depending on it.

There shouldn't be any room in his mind for agonizing over trivial things. Things like whether to go to Brandon's place this weekend. It had become expected—they worked twelve-hour days on the weekends toward getting the Smiths' cottage rebuilt. More, he had no excuse to not go. But ever since that uncomfortably convicting Easter weekend a few weeks back, Brayden couldn't help but agonize, not to mention avoid Brandon, Megan, the Alexanders, and the Smiths. Particularly Audrey.

He'd gone way too far with Audrey. Brandon had been right—Audrey was young, and she looked at him like he was her champion come out of a romance novel. Brayden had used her.

He'd used her.

She was a good girl. A kind girl. Smart and gentle, and aside from her taking up with Brayden, a compliant girl. What kind of a man did a thing like that to a sweet, innocent girl like Audrey Smith?

Not a Murphy. Who even was he?

Fisting the tennis ball, Brayden squeezed until his knuckles turned white, then fired it across the room. It flew back at him, and he snagged it out of the air. Growling a curse unbecoming his heritage, he clenched the ball again.

"Just end it and move on." His advice fell into the silent room as a flat, uninspiring sound that was absorbed into nothingness before it could have much effect.

He should have ended it months ago, when Brandon had suggested it. Well, more like demanded it, which played into Brayden's stubbornness against the idea. Now? Things were complicated, though Brayden wasn't entirely sure why. People broke up all the time, even after they'd slept together.

Wasn't that uncommon—take him and Leah, for example.

But for some reason, this time *just end it* felt wrong. Like . . . like he owed Audrey more. Better.

Because she was so young? Or because she adored him, more so than Leah ever had, and even if he couldn't claim that he loved her, he did enjoy that?

With a fling of his right arm, the tennis ball went soaring again. His aim was off though, and it hit the lamp sitting on the edge of his dresser. The shade toppled to the side and then pulled the stand in its trajectory. Before he could jump off the bed and intervene on gravity's pull, the glass of the bowl and the lightbulb met the hardwood planks.

A shattered pottery and glass mess skidded across the floor.

Not what he'd intended. Seemed the story of his life.

~~ele~~

Audrey had no idea if Brayden would show this weekend. He hadn't in the previous two, and she hadn't had the heart or the gumption to text him. Part of her really didn't want to see him. The scared part that didn't want to say out loud what that pregnancy test had proclaimed.

She had to tell him though, and she'd do it in person.

A mild surge of nausea swam through her as she sat in a quiet corner of the Alexanders' garden, phone tight in her fist. The stone bench she'd lowered onto was chilly, with late April's fickle temps. Today had been overcast and hinted more at winter's remnants than spring's promise, which seemed fitting.

How was she going to go forward in life now?

Swallowing against the urge to be sick, Megan squeezed her eyes shut. *God, You must be so disappointed in me. I'm sorry. I'm so, so sorry.*

The chill of stone beneath her seeped through the back of her jeans. Bracing one hand against that cold stability, Audrey opened her eyes and took in the manicured landscape before her. Lovely pink heads of various hues bobbed in a chilly breeze. Had it only been last year she and Megan had been out here clipping blossoms and commiserating about how the handsome Brandon Murphy was impossibly serious? Just a year before, had she'd been secretly wondering what on earth was wrong with her friend, who was like a sister, that Megan wouldn't even give Brandon a chance? Maybe had even had a small crush on the man herself?

Despite his stern demeanor, Brandon had proven himself to be exactly what Mrs. Alexander had proclaimed him: a good man. A much better man than Marcus Kensington could ever hope to be. Audrey had wondered why Megan refused to see that. She'd also wondered how it was possible for Megan not to be swept away, at least a little bit, by his looks. The woodsman who had been sent as Megan's arranged fiancé was some kind of particular handsome.

So much had changed in twelve months.

Megan was now the blissfully happy Mrs. Brandon Murphy. And Audrey . . .

A cry trembled through her middle, threatening escape. Audrey willed it back while clutching an arm around her middle.

Brayden wasn't like Brandon, no matter how much Audrey had hoped he would be.

"Audrey?"

Sucking in a quick breath, Audrey jolted her posture straight and searched for Megan. By the sound of her voice, she should be rounding the large berm, which was currently under waves of blooming tulips.

"There you are. Your mom said you were out here." Megan stepped toward her across the shortly mowed grass, her smile almost as brilliant as the simple diamond winking from her ring finger. As she neared, however, that grin faded and her eyebrows folded inward. "Are you okay?"

"Sure." Audrey cleared her voice. "It's Friday afternoon, so of course I'm okay. I'm good."

Concern creased Megan's expression deeper. "You're good?"

"Yep. Totally good. Yay for the weekend, right?" She wasn't usually this much of a jabber-box. Might be why Megan looked at her like she wasn't sure who was sitting there just then.

Megan licked her lips, ran her hands down her dark-wash jeans, and then lowered onto the bench next to Audrey, all the while studying her. "Brandon said that Brayden is coming this weekend."

Boxing the layers of emotions that news dumped in her chest, Audrey went for an impassive expression. "Did he?"

"He did. Maybe you already knew that though, hmm?"

"Nope."

"No? You haven't talked to him this week?"

"Nope."

"Audrey." Megan shifted toward Audrey until their knees touched. "What's happened, hon? You've been so off the past few weeks. Since Easter."

"I just told you. I'm fine. I'm good."

"You're lying." She held her with a flat, unflinching stare.

Audrey looked away, one part desperate to spill her secret to her friend, and the other part terrified of the inevitable day when she wouldn't be able to keep it from her any longer. What would Megan do? Brayden was her brother-in-law now. Where would that leave their relationship? And what about Brandon? While Audrey had held a secret crush on the man at one time, now he'd become like the big brother she'd never had, and Audrey had so much respect for him. Even if he had been overbearing when he'd insisted that she be careful when it came to his younger brother.

She should have listened.

"What has Brayden done?" A cool demand made Megan's voice edgy.

Hadn't just been Brayden. Audrey swallowed hard and blinked against the warm moisture in her eyes, still refusing to look at Megan.

"I can tell Brandon to tell him not to come."

"No." That stifled cry nearly broke free. Audrey drew in a breath, then forced her eyes to Megan's. "No. I need to see him. Even if it's just this one last time."

"Audrey, what's—"

"Please don't ask me right now, Meg."

For several thudding heartbeats, silence weighed the space between them. Then Megan reached for Audrey's hand. Warm and gentle, her fingers enclosed around Audrey's. "You're the sister of my heart, Audrey. I do hope, after what we've been through this year, that you know that. That I've earned your trust despite my past failures."

Pressing her lips together, Audrey nodded. It was all she could manage.

"Whatever this is, don't do it alone forever. Okay?"

"'Kay," she whispered.

Megan pulled her in close and then wrapped her in a two-armed hug. "I got you. No matter what, I've got you."

There was that—a small solace in a friend who wouldn't abandon her.

Audrey hoped.

Chapter Three

(IN WHICH HARD THINGS MUST BE FACED)

Brayden shouldered his bag after he yanked it from the backseat of his sedan and pivoted on the packed river rock that made up the surface of the drive. His gaze traveled from the driveway to the flagstone path, up the steps to the covered front porch and to the teal front door. If anyone had landed on their feet in life, it'd been Brandon. He'd won the destiny lottery. A letter in the mail asking him to come, take the role of fiancé to a beautiful heiress, and now all of this was Brandon's. No cost. No effort. Just . . . luck.

His overly serious, too stern, and somewhat condescending brother had all the luck.

That hard burn clenched in Brayden's chest. But never mind that. Brayden had a plan for his life. Medical school, then residency. Then he'd go back to Sugar Pine as a general practitioner. He'd be the most successful of the Murphy brothers. Respect. Status. He'd have it all. Without luck.

Brandon could have his arranged marriage. Whatever. Brayden would *earn* his fortune, and he wouldn't be beholden to a father-in-law to maintain it. Nor would he be dependent on his wife's trust fund.

If he ever had a wife.

Not an if. He would. Eventually. Leah could enjoy her life as an army wife, and good luck with that. They could have had it all, together. But she'd made her choice.

With the sound of rocks underfoot, Brayden pushed down the bitterness that burned in his gut and moved up the walkway. Just as he stepped up the first riser, that teal front door swept open wide, and his older brother's brawny frame filled the void between porch and house. Brandon pushed a shoulder against the doorframe and crossed his arms. "How was the drive?"

"Uneventful."

"That's good."

Brayden closed the distance, and Brandon leaned off the frame and moved to allow entry. "Been a few weeks since you've come. Everything okay?"

Man. Couldn't even let him through the doorway before the interrogation began. "Studying. Med school's not a cakewalk."

"I'll bet not."

Brandon wouldn't know. He hadn't even finished college. Chose a blue-collar life of physical labor. Even still, here he was. Living the life. Because of luck.

After four steps inside, Brayden paused and turned to his brother, grabbing the stair railing as he did so. "Guest room, same as always?"

"Yeah. Meg said she put clean towels in the wardrobe. Dinner's at the big house tonight. We eat in about half an hour."

He'd have to claim a headache to get out of that one. Two weeks, a couple hours' drive, and he still wasn't ready to face Audrey. Not when he'd settled on cutting ties and moving on.

He *had* settled on it. No matter the heartburn that the plan flared. It was just the way things were gonna be. She'd get over it, move on. She was, after all, young. Beautiful. Sweet. Smart.

She gave you everything, and you know it mattered to her.

That fire in his middle flared.

Be a better man.

Brandon rubbed his forehead and cleared his throat. "Think I'm gonna take a pass on dinner tonight. My head's splitting wide open."

"Drink enough water?"

Stifling a groan, he shot Brandon a glare. "I am in med school."

"Right." Brandon narrowed a pinched gaze on him. "Sorry about the headache. There's some ibuprofen in the bathroom cabinet, and if you do get hungry, I think there are some leftovers in the fridge."

Nodding, Brayden turned to climb the stairs.

"Bray."

"What?" his tone bit, and he knew it. Didn't care much though.

"Not now, but we need to talk."

"About what?"

"Audrey."

"Pretty sure we've had that talk. Several times. Always ends the same—stay out of it. It's not your business who I date."

"Megan found her pretty upset this afternoon. Says that you two haven't been talking."

"Stay out of it." He flung a piercing glare over his shoulder. "Anyway, weren't you the one telling me all this time to leave her alone?"

A single nod accompanied Brandon's unflinching stare. "I did. But be a man about it. You owe her at least that." Brandon's lips fell in a hard line.

Brayden whipped his gaze away and stomped up the stairs, battling that burn in his chest and anger that made his hands shake. He did owe Audrey a conversation. Likely, he owed her more than that, but he couldn't give anything else. But Brandon didn't know the details, and he didn't need to. Wasn't his business, and why was he always all up in Brayden's stuff anyway? It was like he thought of the pair of them, he was the only responsible one. Couldn't he just let Brayden live his own dang life?

Doing a good job of it, aren't you?

A real headache stabbed near his eyes as that deprecating thought pierced through. Yeah, he was doing a decent job of living, thank you very much. He'd made it through college, hadn't he? Scored well enough on the MCAT to get into medical school? He was doing all right for himself, and it'd be nice if one of his plethora of brothers would notice now and then, rather than always treating him like the helpless little brother they needed to boss.

Crossing into the guest room he'd slept in several times before, Brayden kicked the lower part of the door with his Cons and strode toward the bed, the thud of the door shutting behind him. Likely Brandon thought he was acting like a teenage brat throwing a fit, hearing the smack of that door.

Is he wrong?

Ugh. Get out of his head already. Wasn't he there, voluntarily giving his time to work on a house, even though he hated construction? Some credit was due.

Now at the bedside, he slid his bag from his shoulder and dropped onto the mattress. Fingers forking into his hair as the pain behind his eyes spread deeper into his brain, Brayden found his reflection in the mirrored wardrobe. He had the Murphy build and looks. Most of the boys did—they took after their father. Brown eyes—Brayden's were dark, like Brandon's—thick dark hair. Average height, but stockier frames. Again, he and Brandon shared the bulkier build of all the boys. Actually, he and Brandon could pass as twins, and had often been mistaken for being so.

One of the reasons Audrey had immediately taken to Brayden, he was certain. First time he'd met her nearly a year before, he'd come around the side of the Alexanders' massive house on the path that led to the backyard, following Brandon. He'd watched while Megan looked only at her arranged fiancé, barely glancing at Brayden at all, and Audrey . . .

She'd set a look on Brandon that was admiration. Clearly she'd had a crush on her friend's intended. Then she looked at Brayden. Eyes widened, she took him in with surprise, quickly followed by a grin that seemed to say *one for me too.* How was he supposed to resist that?

He hadn't. And he'd fully enjoyed Audrey's admiration. True, he also had come to find that she was smart and kind and possessed a quiet, subtle sense of humor that was like discovering a hidden gem where one hadn't even thought to look. All of that made coming back to her an easy choice—even if it did trigger Brandon's overbearing bossy side.

Truth was, he really did like Audrey.

But Audrey wasn't Leah. She wasn't all outgoing and audacious. Wasn't the reckless daredevil type. Certainly wasn't a wild child that would break all the rules with him, laughing as they went.

Well, she *had* broken some boundaries with him.

With Leah, there hadn't been regret. There'd had been justification and toss all caution to the wind.

Crossing lines with Audrey made him feel like . . . like a thief. Like maybe he deserved Brandon's condescending scowls.

Brayden didn't like that feeling.

"Ugh." With that growl, he spun away from his reflection and made for the attached bathroom. He refused to meet his own scowl in the mirror above the sink as he opened the medicine cabinet. Snatching his quarry, he shook three pills into his palm, tossed them into his mouth, and swallowed.

He'd end this whole mess this weekend, and then move on. Brandon would still glower at him, but at least he wouldn't feel like he was likely to mess up Audrey's life.

They could go their separate ways, no harm done.

—ele—

Audrey forced herself to eat half of her potato soup, doing so while remaining quiet and barely looking up. The people around her conversed warmly, as they usually did. Mom and Dad, the Alexanders, and the newly wedded Murphys. All blissful and happy, their lives undisrupted.

Her mind and body were chaos in the midst of their peace.

Brayden had begged off dinner. Likely because he and Brandon had crossed words upon his arrival. An assumption on Audrey's part, but one founded in recent history. As she'd come to know Brayden the past several months, she'd found one unmoving fact about the man: he was nothing like Brandon and resented that people thought otherwise. Went out of his way, in fact, to be the opposite of his older brother.

Audrey could understand that on some level. While she'd always loved Megan, there were definitely things about Meg that Audrey didn't want to mimic. Also, with Brayden, she liked that he wasn't so stern and severe. Brayden was carefree and fun. He was the drive with the top down and stand up on the seat while he was doing so type. While she wasn't exactly the wild type herself, she liked Brayden's live-it-up attitude.

Usually.

He made her laugh. Not to mention, breathlessly heady.

Heat rushed to her face as she thought on those passionate kisses.

As her stomach rolled miserably, Audrey put her spoon into her half-finished soup and reached for the glass of ice water. The chilled liquid sliding down her throat did little to cool her cheeks, nor did it settle her stomach.

"You okay, Audrey?" Across the table, Mom tipped her head to one side, a worried expression creasing her brow.

Audrey blew out a slow breath. "I'm not feeling great."

"You look pale."

Nodding, Audrey scooched her chair back. "I think I'm done." She turned to Mrs. Alexander. "I'm sorry, but will you excuse me?"

Next to Audrey, Mrs. Alexander reached for her hand and squeezed. "Of course. I hope you're not sick."

"I'm sure it'll pass." Again, she glanced at her mother, though she could barely make eye contact. "The soup is delicious, Mom. Save me some?"

"Of course, hon. Let me know if you need me to bring something up to you later."

Audrey gave her a silent nod and then slipped away. Behind her, she felt the eyes of the others watching her go. Particularly, she felt Megan watching her as she moved up the stairs.

Whatever this is, don't do it alone.

A rebel tear slipped onto her nose. Megan likely knew the truth, and she all but told Audrey that she'd go through this with her. But it wasn't Megan she wanted at her side.

She wanted Brayden. Wanted his smile, his delight. Wanted his love. Too late, she'd realized that was a fantasy. Point of fact: he'd been silent the past few weeks. And tonight? She was willing to bet a headache was nothing more than a flimsy excuse. Brayden was avoiding her. Which made telling him the truth all the worse.

She dreaded it.

As she shut the door to her room, Audrey leaned back and shut her eyes. *I can't do this, God.*

How could she have let this happen? How could she have given *everything*—heart and body—to a man who had never said he loved her? Who never would? How had she become *this* girl?

There were no answers. Only tears, and a hollowness that grew with each sniff. Perhaps once she told him, she'd begin to recover. Once it was out there, she'd start to accept the reality and figure out how to live with it.

Maybe he'll surprise you.

There was the problem right there. She kept clinging to a hope she knew to be impossible, and once she told him, he'd shatter all illusions. She'd only be left with the iron truth that had been there all along. She wasn't Leah, and Brayden didn't love her.

It was time to face that.

Audrey slid her hand to grip the cold knob on the door at her back. *Face it.* Swiping away the tears, she let herself back out of her room, moved toward the back stairway, and then took herself out of the house. She had a ten-minute walk in which she could build up her courage. Ten minutes, and then she'd face it.

She'd face *him*.

And then . . .

Then her heart would fall to pieces all over again.

Chapter Four

(IN WHICH DECISIONS MUST BE MADE)

Brayden had ignored the knock on the front door. But he couldn't ignore the text message that had just flashed on his phone.

It's just me. I need to talk to you.

So, Audrey was going to be the bigger person. He sat up on the couch, covered his face with one hand, and pushed away the smallness that encroached around him. Brandon had been right, blast it. She deserved for Brayden to act like a man about this. Instead, he'd avoided her.

But only because he didn't want to do this with an audience. Apparently she didn't either, because she'd obviously snuck away from the big house while the others were still at dinner. Very *not* Audrey-esque. She was a good person, close to her family, and not one to sneak or lie.

Not like him.

She would be better off without him, anyway. A few tears and some resentment probably, and Audrey would get over him and find someone more suited to her guileless personality. Time would heal, and she'd be glad he broke things off.

Even so, Brayden felt like a rat. Blowing out a breath, he reached for the door and pulled it open, fixing a grin he'd practiced for many years as he did so. Charm was easier than authenticity.

That facade faded as she turned toward the door, her arms wrapped around herself in uncertainty, her face pale, and her eyes weepy.

Great. This was already a scene, and he hadn't even said anything yet.

"Audrey."

Her lips pressed tight, and he could see her swallow. "We need to talk. Can I come in?"

Nodding, he tugged the door open wider. She passed in front of him, waited for the entry to close, and then hugged herself tighter.

"Look," he started, feeling immediately defensive. "The thing is—"

"The thing is—"

His lips snapped shut. Audrey wasn't the type to interrupt. Nor was she the unsmiling, stern-faced type.

"—I'm pregnant."

Suddenly the room seemed void of oxygen. Audrey held a look on him, one that was pleading and uncertain, while he stood there suffocating and paralyzed. He had no idea how long they remained as statues, unable to breathe or move or—in his case—think. It felt eternal, but sooner than he was ready, she looked toward the door and sniffed.

"That's all, I guess. Now you know." She moved to leave, swiping her cheek as she did so.

"Wait." Brayden reached for her arm. He had no idea what he thought he was going to say or do next. But she couldn't just leave. Not after that.

Fragmented hope flickered in her eyes as she looked up at him. "Wait? For what, Brayden?"

"I—" He had no idea. Pregnant? The possibility had never once crossed his mind. Why it wouldn't, he now had no idea. He was, after all, in medical school. He did have a grasp on basic biology and procreation. But . . .

But.

"Just, let me process." He rubbed his jaw as the thoughts that had stalled began to race. Pregnant! How could he cut things off now? Audrey had plans for her life. Most immediate of those was to graduate from high school. God! He'd gotten a high school girl pregnant. What had he been thinking?

What would she do? Nursing school was next on her plans. With a baby? Would that work? What would *he* do?

Dad would kill him. Mom would weep. He was gonna be the ultimate Murphy failure.

Did they have to know?

"How long do you need to process this, Brayden?" Audrey folded her arms and tipped a frown at him. "We let things go too far and made a baby. Of the two of us, you should have a better understanding of that. You're going to be a doctor. This shouldn't be too hard to process."

Brayden drew back, shock filling him. Audrey wasn't like this. Not usually. Only one other time had he witnessed her being snippy, and that had been with Megan. Truthfully, Megan had deserved it. She'd acted so Beverly Hills toward Audrey. All rich and uppity. In his eyes, Audrey had been completely justified.

Was she justified now? Did *he* deserve her snippiness?

Failure wrung out like sour milk within him. Here he'd been prepared to dump her. Had decided he was done indulging himself in the pleasant distraction she'd provided. Clean break? Not possible now.

Brayden swallowed back the acrid taste in his mouth. "I understand the concept," he whispered low. "Processing the reality is a little more difficult. How long have you known?"

"Two weeks." Her gaze hardened further. "Almost the exact amount of time you've ignored me."

"I wasn't ignoring you." He felt the wince twitch on his brow. *Liar.*

"No?"

"I have finals . . ."

"Me too. Try studying when your stomach refuses to settle and all you can think about in between vomiting is how badly you've messed up your life."

He couldn't imagine. His own thoughts had been consumed by the guilt that had latched in his conscience that Easter morning. That had been difficult enough to work around. Ache for her drained the defensiveness that had been pooling, and he stepped closer, once again cupping her arm in his palm. "You could have called me."

Eyes sliding shut, she was obviously battling for self-control. And losing. Brayden slipped his hand around her back and gently pulled her against him. The fight drained from her, and she pressed her forehead into his chest. His hold around her firmed as she cried.

This changed everything. But he still didn't know what to do. "Have you told anyone else?"

The movement of her head indicated no. "Everyone will think so much less of me."

He knew that worry intimately. How would he ever hope to live up to the Murphy name now?

Maybe no one needed to know. The idea took root before the thought even fully formed. He could fix this.

Would Audrey agree though? Maybe. Probably—what else was she going to do? But she was pretty upset with him just now. Might need some delicate handling. Precision timing. The right place, right time.

Inching back, he took her shoulders, thumbs brushing her collarbone until she looked up at him. Misery and helplessness bled in those eyes that were usually a merry shade of green. She'd agree. If he did it right.

"Listen." He lifted one hand and cupped her wet cheek with it. "It's going to be okay."

Disbelief read loud and clear as her expression puckered into another sob. "I don't see how."

Brayden leaned down and pressed a kiss to that furrowed brow. "It will. Let's just keep this between us for now though. Okay?"

A ragged breath eased from her frame, blowing hot against his neck. She didn't answer.

"Just let me do some thinking. Some checking." He wrapped her in another embrace and held her firm. "It's going to be okay. Trust me."

After a long, hollow pause, in which he keenly felt her doubt, Audrey slipped her arms around him and held. Still, no answer.

She didn't trust him. He hadn't given her a reason to.

Great. Even to her—this girl who had spent nearly the past year gazing at him as if he was Captain America and had gone along with whatever he was up for—Brayden was an untrustworthy failure.

That did not bode well.

~ele~

The Alexanders' backyard had become a fairy land of crabapple trees in bloom and twinkling lights. Dotting the spring-green grass, there were tables covered with white cloths and boasting vases of blooms, fresh cut from the bursting landscape. On the flagstone patio, near the gurgling water feature, a long table had been positioned as the focal point. Atop its white cloth and spacing the three large bouquets, was a chocolate fountain surrounded by marshmallows, fruit, and graham crackers, a tower of decadent vanilla-caramel cupcakes (Audrey's favorite), and a large crystal punch bowl heaped full of homemade ice cream. The balloon arch over the head table sported a banner that had been specially ordered for this occasion. *Congratulations Audrey!*

Megan had been giddy when she'd led Audrey out of the front of the house and around the stepping path that flanked the side. "You didn't peek while you were upstairs, did you?"

For the first time in a month, Audrey giggled. "No, Meg. I promised I wouldn't, and I didn't."

They'd paused at the corner of the house. "Close your eyes," Megan demanded.

Audrey did, and Megan had gripped her hand and led her forward. At the sound of applause, she'd opened her eyes and found this. All of this beauty and friends and family there to celebrate her graduation. Tears had burned the corners of her eyes. She'd felt terribly unworthy of such attention and celebration. Especially now.

A wave of nausea rushed over her as she stood there, taking in this fairy-land gift that had been planned and executed by Megan, who remained at her side, hand still gripping hers. Audrey stepped back, nearly stumbling, as this surge was particularly strong.

Megan held her firm and then slipped her arm around Audrey's waist. "You okay?"

"Yeah." Audrey focused on the water feature, demanding that her world stabilize. She'd kept her promise to Brayden—hadn't told anyone their secret. Not even Megan, though she worried her friend had already guessed. But if Audrey went down now, she might not have that option of concealment anymore. "This is so overwhelming, is all. You shouldn't have done all this for me."

"Yes, I should have." Megan squeezed. "I'm so proud of you Audrey. I know it's been such a rough year, with your house burning down and getting hurt and needing surgery. But look at you! Graduating with honors and nursing-school bound. You are an overcomer, my friend."

A sob caught in Audrey's throat. Megan had worked so hard over the past many months to prove herself Audrey's true friend. Their fallout the previous summer had really shaken Megan up, and Audrey couldn't deny how much Megan had changed since then. Since meeting Brandon. She'd grown so much as a person, becoming stable, kinder, and full of purpose. Growing into the person Megan had always had the potential to be.

Truthfully, their fallout had been partly on Audrey's shoulders too—when it had come to Brayden, Megan had had Audrey's best at heart when she'd warned her away from her then-fiancé's brother. Audrey could see that clearly now.

Too little too late.

But she couldn't dwell on that right now. She'd break down and fall apart, right there in the middle of this lovely graduation party Megan had gifted her. All the pieces that had shattered inside of her would spill out for all to see.

No. She would not allow that. She'd press through this, clinging to a that wispy bit of trust she'd invented that Brayden would make good on his claim: that everything would be okay.

As if it could be.

Audrey cleared her throat and squeezed Megan back. "Thank you for this, Meg. It's amazing."

A wide smile filled Megan's expression, and she leaned to peck Audrey on the cheek. "Enjoy everything. You deserve it. But I promise I won't let this go too late. I know how people can wear you out." Winking, she led Audrey to the long table of rich desserts. "Fortify yourself now. You have many fans, and everyone wants to congratulate you."

Her fingers shook as Audrey reached for a cupcake. She doubted she'd be able to get the decadence into her stomach, but if she set it on a plate and had it in hand while she visited, perhaps no one would catch on.

Megan hadn't been exaggerating—a lot of people were milling around the Alexanders' backyard. Many from church. Some from school. A few neighbors. All of them wanted to hug Audrey and tell her well done. Conspicuously, Brayden was not among them. Audrey told herself that was a relief—and likely a product of Megan not inviting her brother-in-law.

An hour and a half into the evening, Audrey wanted to duck inside the house for a few minutes of quiet with no one touching her. She could say she needed the restroom. That wouldn't look suspicious.

The plated cupcake still in hand, Audrey turned from the middle of the yard. But when her vision stopped on the dark-haired man who had just come down the flagstone steps from the raised patio, she stopped dead. Her breath caught as those familiar dark eyes landed on her. Dressed in a suit, a bouquet of white roses in hand, Brayden looked as handsome as anyone she'd ever imagined. And darn, but the man could make her knees turn to jelly.

Or maybe that was just her current condition.

Brayden held her gaze as he strode forward and smiled. It seemed like a mask. Like something he'd work up before stepping onto a stage. He stopped in front of her, cupped her shoulder with his empty hand, and leaned to kiss her cheek. "Hi."

"Hi." Audrey nearly choked on that solo syllable. "I didn't know you were here."

"I meant for it to be a surprise." One lid dropped, and he passed the flowers to her. The breath that brushed by her nose as he spoke smelled of mint schnapps. "Congratulations."

An hour and a half late to the party. She could guess why. But Brayden seemed steady, in full command of himself.

"Thanks." Moistening her lips, Audrey wondered how many of the guests were staring at them in that moment. Intense discomfort crawled over her. She didn't like attention. Not like this. Didn't Brayden know that?

She was certain at some point she'd told him.

One large hand surrounded hers and then lifted it to his lips. "I have another surprise." For one long moment, Brayden stalled. Audrey thought she saw a flicker of panic pass through his gaze. But then that mask locked back into place, and he—

Oh no. What was he doing? Audrey's heart hammered, and she froze.

Brayden planted a knee into the grass, swept a look around them, and cleared his throat. "I think it's time everyone knows where I stand." He chuckled. "Or, at the moment, kneel."

Audrey shook, and there was no way Brayden didn't know it. Not with her hand still clasped in his. He wasn't . . . couldn't be . . .

"Audrey Smith, you and I have a future. I don't think we should wait around to start it. Will you marry me?"

Silence crashed around her, and breathing seemed impossible. Every eye bored into her from all sides, waiting.

What would she say?

Marry Brayden? This was his plan? Why hadn't he talked to her about it? It'd been two weeks since she'd told him about the baby. He'd called her here and there, checking in. *How are you feeling? You haven't said anything, right? It's going to work out. Trust me.*

Nowhere in those conversations that frankly had seemed forced at best had Brayden mentioned anything about marriage. How could he spring this on her right there in the middle of everything and everyone?

"Audrey? You're making me a little nervous here." He chuckled again. It sounded hollow. "You gonna marry me?"

"Yes." It came out on a long-held breath, shocking her as much as it did anyone. But what other option did she have, standing there trembling, Brayden staring up at her, and everyone around them watching the whole thing go down?

The grin she knew well—an *I got my way* smirk that up until that moment she'd considered cute—curved his mouth, and he slipped a diamond ring on her finger. In fluid motion, Brayden stood and swept her into an embrace.

Audrey nearly hyperventilated against him. Had that just happened? Had she just agreed to marry Brayden? She squeezed her eyes shut.

She'd been fairly certain she loved him the past few months. But he . . .

He proposed.

Because she was pregnant.

He said to trust him. Maybe try that.

It felt wrong.

Around them, the gathering murmured, as if no one knew exactly what to do. Then someone clapped, and others followed. Audrey would have bet that her parents were not among those applauding. She shook violently as he held her close.

"It's gonna be okay, Audrey." Brayden's warm breath fanned against her ear as he whispered.

She wished desperately she could believe him.

Chapter Five

(IN WHICH QUESTIONS MUST BE ADDRESSED)

"I'm not saying no." Across the large office where Mr. Alexander conducted his business affairs, Tim Smith continued to frown. The man's furrowed brow hadn't relaxed from the moment his gaze had collided with Brayden's, and that had been hours before, while the party was still in full swing.

Brayden sure could make an entrance.

Tense silence had taken on a whole new meaning as Brayden had waited on bended knee for Audrey to answer his proposal, and it hadn't eased much when she'd said yes. Everyone had been dumbfounded, none more than the girl he'd asked to marry him. And the variety of her shock wasn't on the *thrilled* spectrum. In truth, Audrey had looked like a cornered kitten, terrified and helpless.

Though he'd planned his proposal with precise intention and had picked a situation in which he was certain she wouldn't bring up all the reasons this was not a good idea, Brayden hadn't expected Audrey's drawn-out hesitation, nor had he been prepared for her to look at him as if he'd trapped her. As that thought rolled through his mind, a surge of resentment surfaced. He was doing the right thing by her. How could she give him that pinched expression that said she felt betrayed?

Hours past that moment, the impression of her disapproval still had him riled.

The upwelling of self-defense had him straightening his posture as he refocused on the only other man in the room. "You're not saying yes either. But I'm not sure how much that's going to carry weight. Audrey said yes."

"She just graduated from high school."

A queasy knot twisted in his gut. Brayden ignored it. "She's an adult, and she knows her own mind."

Tim Smith ran both hands down his face and let out a long sigh. "Brayden, I'm her father." He settled a tired, hurt-filled look on Brayden. As the silence extended, that expression hardened into anger as he gripped the leather chair in front of him. "I would think that you'd respect me enough as her father to listen. Though I don't know why. You didn't even approach me about this. She's young. She's innocent. She's my *daughter*! I thought you Murphy men were supposed to be the good sort?"

You're not good enough for her, even if your last name is Murphy. Tim might as well have said it, as Brayden heard the accusation loud and clear.

"This is just because I didn't ask you first? That's ridiculous."

"You know it's not, but it's certainly part of it. Respect, Brayden. That's what we're talking about here. How can I know that you'll respect my daughter as your wife when you clearly don't respect me?" Tim pushed off the back of the chair and strode forward, fire blazing in his stare. "This has all the marks of arrogance. You sprung this on all of us, including Audrey, and you think we should simply fawn at you with delight and gratitude?" A flat hand slashed the air as Tim stopped in front of him. "No. I want the best for my little girl, even if she is a merely a gardener's daughter."

Brayden drew back, part in surprise at Tim's angry outburst. The man had always struck Brayden as a pacifist. Rather meek and too easygoing to raise a fuss. Audrey had inherited a large part of that personality trait—that had been one of the reasons Brayden had found solace with her. She wasn't prone to arguing. Went with the flow.

But she'd revealed a layer beneath that, hadn't she? And now Brayden saw it in her father too. Tim was no pushover.

Well, neither was Brayden, and he had reasons to see this through. "Is that what you think? I look down on you, on Audrey, because of your occupation? As if I should care! My dad is blue-collar too, and no one in this current world cares one way or another about it."

"You thought she was easy prey. Just a gooey-eyed girl who would do whatever you asked."

"Prey?" The offended edge of Brayden's voice was not forced. Though he might not have been entirely honorable in this relationship with Audrey, he wasn't a predator.

"She has a future, Brayden Murphy. She's a smart girl. A good girl."

"I know!" Brayden's hands shook as he rolled fists at his side. "I know all of that. Why do you think I want to be in her future?"

Seriously? Had all of that been sincere? The ferocity that fueled his response felt authentic. And yes, he did know those things about Audrey. That she was smart and good and had a future. But those weren't exactly his reasons.

Fraud.

Brayden ignored the condemning voice in his head. He couldn't afford to back down. This was the way things needed to be. He and Audrey would get married, and they'd do it soon. No one needed to know.

No one needed to be ashamed of him.

He looked down to his clenched fists as his angry outburst sank into murky regret. When Brayden finally worked up the courage to glance at Audrey's father, he found the man with his head tipped back, face lined with angst, eyes closed. Though no audible words came out, Tim's lips moved.

Brayden made out the words *according to Your will* before Tim swallowed and lowered his gaze back to him. A praying man, just like Dad.

The blaze of anger had eased in Tim's look, but his brow remained deeply lined. "Let's begin this again." Tim's voice was raw but controlled. "I am not saying no. But I am saying not yet. Let her get a year of nursing school behind her. Let her experience a little more of life. That will allow you to focus on medical school, which I'm sure isn't easy. Adding a wife to it—" He shook his head. "I think it'd be better if you waited."

That'd be a fine, persuasive argument, but there was no time for waiting. "What if that's not what Audrey wants?"

"Audrey is a reasonable girl. Once I talk to her—"

"It's not what she wants. It's not what *we* want."

With a flat-mouthed expression, Tim shook his head. "Sometimes what we want and what is prudent are not the same thing. Sometimes God asks us to wait."

God? He was invoking God in this, like Tim was a heavenly mouthpiece or something?

Sounded like something his own father would say to him. In fact, Brayden would wager that a carbon copy of this conversation would happen in the near future, only Tim would be replaced with Brayden's dad. Couldn't the people in his life just let him make his own decisions? Couldn't they trust that he had his reasons?

God knows the reasons.

A furnace lit in his core. Brayden tried to ignore the scalding heat within. *Trust?*

Again, Brayden attempted to silence the piercing voice in his head. This time, it pushed back. *Trust? You are the last man these people can trust. You've taken what wasn't yours, messed up Audrey's life, and now you're covering your tracks.*

You. Are. Shameful.

What was he supposed to do? Pin a red letter *A* onto his shirt and walk around with it, proclaiming his failure to the world? As if the world at large would care anyway. This little world he lived in—the one created by his pious parents and the excessive expectations of the Alexanders and the Smiths—was a pseudo reality. Most people didn't live by these antiquated standards. Anyway, if he was really as shameful as his guilty conscious proclaimed him to be, he'd walk away from Audrey and leave her to deal with it on her own.

He was trying to do the right thing here, dang it! If only these interfering people would step aside.

Brayden jammed forked fingers into his hair and blew out hot exasperation. "I don't see the point in delay. Audrey and I are going to get married—"

"If only to honor her father, isn't that a good enough reason?" There was the mild man again. Soft spoken, and yet his words delivered a powerful blow.

It would be a good enough reason. Except then everyone would know. *They'll see how short I fall.*

Brayden wasn't going to allow that.

—ell—

Audrey gripped the collar of her coat and held it closed at the neck. The chilly wind coming off the peaks held the bite of snow, heedless that it was May. Didn't help that she felt cold from the inside out. Moving her gaze from those granite monuments of God's power, currently painted in the early morning hues of soft, glowing orange, she studied the swift-flowing waters of the spring melt making the creek wide and wildly white.

The tumult of that current moved in her very soul.

At her side, Brayden scuffed the scattered rocks beneath his boot. She'd asked him to meet her there and had managed to squeak out that she wasn't sure this engagement was the right thing to do. His unhappy silence over the past moments weighed like stone.

"I thought you'd be happy." His voice sounded defensive and sullen.

Audrey turned her face to look at him. He sat, cross-armed and face drawn into a frown, on an oblong boulder that had managed to escape the reach of the flooding waters.

Do you actually want *to marry me?*

She wasn't sure she wanted to hear his answer to that, and the fact that she even had that thought in her head made her want to cry. What girl wanted her one and only romance to go this way?

"You caught me off guard," she said, not able to summon a smile.

"That was the point. To surprise you."

"But you did it front of everyone. Like . . . like . . ." *Like it was a setup. Like that way, she couldn't refuse him, or at least ask him* why *he wanted to marry her all the sudden.* As if she couldn't guess.

"I thought women liked that sort of thing. You know, to be the belle of the ball or whatever."

Audrey couldn't help but hold a *that's dumb* glare on him. "It's like you haven't paid attention to who I am at all. I'm not the kind of girl who likes that sort of attention."

For a moment, Brayden scowled with pure frustration. Or maybe irritation. But as quick as a late-summer storm, his frown cleared away and the classic Brayden charm lifted his mouth. Dark eyes narrowing on her in a way that she found delightfully intense, he rose and strode toward her. Before he closed the gap between them, he took her hand and pressed her palm to his chest. Then he leaned to kiss her forehead. The spot near her eye. Her nose. Those warm, intoxicating lips skimmed her cheekbone and then nipped her ear.

"How about I try again, then, hmm?" His deep, quiet voice and the warmth of his whisper spreading on her skin sent a thrilling shiver down her spine.

Gripping the sweater beneath her palm, Audrey stifled a sigh. This had been her undoing weeks before. He was so . . . so . . .

Brayden turned his face into her neck and began a slow trail of kisses toward her collarbone as he moved her grip from his sweater to the back of his neck. When she tangled her fingers in his thick hair, he palmed her back and pulled her against him.

A blissful, warm fog took over her mind. "Brayden . . ." She breathed his name as if it were holy to her.

"Marry me, Audrey." He moved in search of her mouth as he spoke. Took her lips in a kiss that was more tease than satisfaction. "Say yes."

All thoughts of protest vanished, drowned by this heady sensation that he summoned. The way he held her, kissed her . . . He wanted her. Did that mean he loved her?

This felt like love, even if he'd never said it.

Brayden pulled his mouth from hers only far enough to whisper her name again.

"Yes," she said and then reclaimed those lips with hunger.

She could live a lifetime with this. The way he made her feel right then, that could last. She wanted it to.

Breathless and heart pounding, Audrey pressed herself against him.

"Soon," he demanded, his possessive hold firm.

"Okay."

He took another tour of her face, then neck. A sigh shuddered through her. "I love you, Brayden."

Lifting his head, he paused long enough to look her in the eyes.

And then he kissed her again.

Chapter Six

(IN WHICH AUDREY LIES)

Brayden stared at the exam prep material, though he didn't comprehend the words he was supposed to be studying. Couldn't, dang it. The step 1 exam was less than two weeks away, and not passing was *not* an option. Everything in his future depended on this—and he was keenly aware that he'd already rerouted a significant portion of his future in the past several months.

Hadn't planned on getting married before he finished med school. Truth be told, he hadn't thought to marry Audrey at all—particularly when she was still a few months from turning nineteen.

What had he been thinking these past months? Not of her—not for her best. The moment she'd locked those eyes full of admiration on him, he'd found his consolation for the bitterness Leah had left behind. That was why he'd kept going back to Audrey, pursuing her, even if he hadn't had a future with her in mind.

She restored his ego and had become a gentle refuge for his bruised heart.

So what was he to her? *Her very own Murphy, since she couldn't have Brandon.* That had been one of his justifications as he'd carried on with her. He wasn't Audrey's first choice—Brandon had been.

Still, as Tim had repeatedly pointed out, Audrey was a girl. A kid.

His gut played a mean game of squeezy-queasy as he thought on that, the conversation with her father easily retriggered.

I think it'd be better if you waited.

Too late for that.

And then, quite rudely, Brandon's reaction to the quick engagement also intruded. *"This is no small thing, and Tim has every right to be upset. To tell you to wait. Think things through for once in your life, Bray!"*

Ugh. Brandon the boss. Couldn't he just get lost in his own happily ever after and let Brayden figure out how to make this work?

"Dang it!" Brayden slammed his hand against the waxy page open on the table. He didn't have time for this. This exam was a no-fail situation. These distractions were unacceptable. He needed to focus.

Audrey though . . . How was she today? Still sick? Brayden knew an ever-present fear that someone was going to figure out their secret, with the way Audrey was often pale and dizzy. All the more reason to move on this marriage thing quickly. If they'd just get it over with, maybe his mind wouldn't be so knotted with the tension.

More importantly, he really did worry about *her.* Going through this alone, as she'd been doing, wasn't fair. Brayden didn't want that for her.

They could just elope. Would Audrey do that?

He could convince her. Hadn't he been able to this far? This would take a little more prep work—more than finding a budget ring at a department store and a handful of flowers at a florist. Audrey wouldn't move forward with this unless he showed her he'd thought about the future—*her* future. She'd been accepted into a nursing school on the coast, but that wouldn't work for them.

Pushing the textbook aside, Brayden strode out the door. With only a pause to snag his wallet and car keys, he left his apartment, set on a mission.

Operation Remove All Distractions commenced. Step one: get Audrey into the pre-nursing program connected with the med center.

Step two: marry the girl—with or without her father's blessing.

Then he could study. He could stop worrying about Audrey, because she'd be right there with him. Easing his mind. Then he could get on with his life as he'd intended.

———

Megan looped an arm through Audrey's as they neared the end of the wide driveway to the big house. Audrey's friend had been right—the evening was lovely. She drew in a deep breath of late May air, full of pine, fresh rain, and bursting new life.

"How are you this evening, my friend?" Megan tugged Audrey nearer as they turned toward the riverside guest house—now Megan and Brandon's house—up the road.

New life . . . Audrey resisted the urge to palm the secret growing in her belly. She'd be a mom at nineteen. Would she be any good at it? Obviously, she'd proven herself completely irresponsible, so it didn't seem likely. She certainly wasn't ready to be one. Nor was she truly ready to be a wife. An overwhelming weight of all that had changed in her world pressed hard against her heart.

The need to tell *someone* the things that kept her from sound sleep at night nearly overcame Audrey's promise of secrecy to Brayden. What would Megan say if Audrey confessed all? On one hand, the thought of her friend's shocked disappointment in her made her want to bury everything deep and pretend her life hadn't completely shifted. But on the other . . .

On the other, Megan loved her. Hadn't this past year proven so, more than ever? For all her faults and shortcomings, Megan was intensely loyal. And though she'd gotten lost in some superficial worries, the fact was, Megan was a good person. Not to mention Audrey's best friend.

But Megan was Brandon's wife now. Her loyalties would lie with him first, not Audrey. Being Brayden's older brother—a stern, serious one at that—meant that things between brothers would go south real fast if Brandon found out the truth. After all, Brandon had already not been happy with the way things went between Brayden and Audrey. This could be the death knell to the brothers.

Audrey didn't want to be the reason the Murphy boys fell apart.

"I'm doing well," Audrey answered vaguely. Inaccurately. Nothing in all this turmoil was well with her.

"Are you?"

She felt the weight of Megan's gaze as Audrey watched the tips of her shoes travel against the gravel of the road. "Yes."

"Audrey."

Lifting her chin, she glanced at Megan. Audrey's tongue very nearly betrayed everything at the sight of knowing pity in Megan's blue eyes. "I haven't felt well. Likely just a spring cold. It's getting better." More lies. Audrey wasn't a liar—she hadn't been, anyway. Actually, lying had triggered bad dreams when she was little, which had quickly cured any inclination to do so.

A quiver rattled through her core as she considered what might wait ahead of her in her sleep.

"Are you sure that's what has been going on?" Megan's extended pause felt intentional, as if she was weighing her words carefully.

She knows.

Wouldn't that be a relief?

"Maybe you're worried about the future?" Megan stopped and, with a hand on Audrey's arm, tugged her to a gentle stop too. "About Brayden?"

Audrey rolled her lips inward and stepped back.

"His proposal was sudden, wasn't it? It looked like you hadn't expected it at all. And, Audrey, you're really young."

Searching for the prowess of falsehoods was a new endeavor for Audrey. She wasn't sure she was doing it well at all. "It was a surprise. He wanted it to be that way."

"Hmm." Megan twisted her mouth to one side, disapproval a hint in that expression. "Seemed like he could have picked a more private setting for such an important question."

Her very thoughts. But Audrey wasn't going to admit that.

"Did you feel trapped into saying yes?" Megan closed the gap that Audrey had pried open moments before. "Be honest with me, Audrey. If he's manipulated you into this—"

"No." Heat crept into her cheeks as her thoughts went to the exact opposite answer. Especially as she replayed their private scene the next morning beside the river, where he'd asked her again and had pulled from her a much more willing answer.

Had that been manipulation too? Or had it been true emotion driving him? Either way, she was putty in his hands. A sharp stab jolted in her chest as she remembered his response to her confession of love. Maybe he just couldn't make the words come out? Maybe that kiss was the same thing.

Shouldn't a guy be able to say *I love you* to the girl he'd proposed to?

Shouldn't a girl expect it?

A sense of dread soured in her already uneasy stomach. Audrey ran the tip of her thumb along the thin band holding the flashy diamond Brayden had placed on her ring finger. Rather than bringing confidence, she felt her insides tremble all over again. It wasn't too late to back out.

Then what?

She'd be a single mom, that was what. A single teen mom who had dumped her future for the temporary thrill of a passionate encounter with a guy who couldn't, or wouldn't, say *I love you*. Pathetic.

The now-familiar roll of shame pressed down on her. It was foolish to think that Megan wouldn't be extraordinarily disappointed in her. Not when Audrey was massively disappointed in herself.

"Audrey, is there a reason you're rushing things with him?"

Her face jerked back toward Megan. *She does know!* Rather than relief, defense surged. "You mean besides love?"

"Do you love him?"

"Yes." At least that wasn't a lie. Audrey loved Brayden, despite his flaws that were surfacing fast. That wasn't the question plaguing her, the reason she battled doubt. The better question would be, did Brayden love her?

She silently begged Megan not to ask that.

"Audrey—"

"Please stop, Meg. Don't make this a thing between us again. I know what you think of him. But he's my fiancé now. More, he's your brother-in-law. At least try to like him."

Megan's eyebrows folded in, and her shoulders slumped. "You know I don't want anything to come between us. Not ever again. With all my heart, Audrey, I want the best life for you. This just seems rushed, and you've been off lately." She reached with both hands and took hold of Audrey's clammy fingers. "I am your friend. Nearly your sister. Just know, you can trust me. No matter what. I'm here for you, thick or thin."

Tears threatened to slip past Audrey's defenses. She leaned in to hug Megan so that she wouldn't see the tears glazing Audrey's eyes. "Be happy for me, Meg."

Firm arms wrapped her shoulders. "Are you happy?"

"Yes." Audrey squeezed her eyes shut, certain her sleep would be restless and full of frightening images. *I'm sorry, God. I either lie to Megan or betray Brayden. Which is worse?*

What did it say about the situation that Brayden needed her to lie? Audrey was young, but she knew it wasn't a promising sign.

Even so, she was in too deep.

Chapter Seven

(IN WHICH WHAT IS DONE IS DONE)

Audrey sat in the passenger seat of Brayden's sedan as he drove sixty-five toward the coast. The twisting of her gut made her wince. She squeezed her fingers into fists, and her eyes shut against the pain. Against the backdrop of eighties rock turned low, Brayden's hand covered one of her own.

"You okay?" he asked.

Shaking her head, she reached for the door and gripped the handle. "You need to pull over."

"Uh-oh."

With frantic, jerky motions, Audrey searched for the seat-belt buckle and had it unlatched before Brayden had the car to a full stop. She tried to pop her door open, but it was locked. "Let me out. I need out now!"

The lock popped, and she shoved her way free just in time to empty her stomach onto the roadside ditch.

"Oh boy." Brayden's hand pressed on her shoulder. "Does this still happen a lot?"

"No." She felt nauseous often, but rarely vomited. This bout, Audrey felt certain, wasn't the baby's doing.

His touch drifted away, and then she heard his door open and shut. As her stomach settled marginally, she leaned her elbows against her legs and pressed her head into her quivering hands.

"Come on." Brayden stepped beside her and cupped her arm. "Let's see if a walk will help. Maybe you're a little carsick."

That was not it either.

Audrey let him tug her up and lead her a few steps from the car before she stopped and burst into tears. "I can't do this, Brayden."

"What?" He turned her and rested his hands on her shoulders. "Do what?"

As if he couldn't figure out what she meant. "My parents are going to be so hurt. This is . . . it's sketchy. We shouldn't have to sneak away to get married."

"Audrey." A pause settled between them, and then he sighed. "I'll admit, it's not what I pictured for my wedding day either. But we can't wait for your dad to come around."

"We could tell them the truth."

"Do you really want to do that?" His ace, one he'd played the week before when he'd come to visit and to lay out his plans.

His plans. He'd lined everything up perfectly—she could hardly argue. She'd be set in the pre-nursing program. He'd visited with the powers that be, made sure there wouldn't be a problem with her enrollment. How did he possess so much persuasion? They'd get married at a courthouse, have a quick honeymoon on the coast, then take a couple days to pack her things and move her to his apartment.

"It's not going to be complicated," he had said. Then he'd grinned that charming grin. *"Marrying you might be the easiest thing I've done in my adult life."*

She'd not been sure that was a compliment. She'd also not been able to argue. Because, to the point he'd just made, she didn't want to confess to her parents any more than he did his.

In her silence alongside the highway, Brayden cupped her face, tipped it up so she'd look at him, and rubbed his thumb along the trail of tears near her nose. "It's going to be okay."

A phrase he kept repeating.

"How do you know?"

"Because once we get married, no one can argue with us."

"That's not everything that's wrong."

"We'll figure it out."

Audrey bit her lip. Framing her face with both hands, Brayden lowered his mouth to kiss her. She ducked away. "I just threw up."

A low chuckle accompanied the brush of his thumb over her top lip. "You did do that. Thanks for saving me."

Managing a lopsided grin, Audrey turned back toward the still-running car. Brayden gripped her hand and led her to it. At the door, she stopped and looked up at him. "Brayden?"

"Yep?"

"Do you—" Her gut twisted. She already knew the answer. If he said it out loud, she wouldn't be able to follow through with this.

Maybe after some time . . . maybe she could make him happy.

"Audrey? You still with me?"

She shook out of her vacant stare across the road and found his eyes again. He looked at her with confident expectation. But not love.

Who married a man who didn't love her?

A desperate woman, that was who. Or, in her case, a foolish girl.

"Are you really sure?"

The sigh he heaved was long and tipped toward exasperation. "I'm really sure. I wouldn't have gone to all the effort to make things as easy as possible for you if I wasn't sure."

That had been kind, hadn't it? Brayden had taken care of the details for her, made sure the transition from high school grad to Mrs. Murphy, pre-nursing student and almost mom, would be seamless.

"The courthouse closes at five." Brayden released her hand and nudged her toward the car.

It's going to be okay. As they pulled back onto the road and continued toward matrimony by five, Audrey adopted Brayden's declaration and tried to believe it for herself. As long as she could keep her stomach from misbehaving, she'd get through this.

Then, perhaps, the hardest part of all this would be behind them. She could figure out how to be a good wife and how to make Brayden love her.

That didn't seem too farfetched. After all, she'd have a lifetime to do it.

~ *ele* ~

Brayden stared at the beach as the steel-gray waves rose to white caps against the solemn sky. The cold wind assaulting his face smelled of salt, seaweed, and fish and sent a wave of goosebumps down his arms. He glanced down at the strawberry-blonde at his side. Audrey's curls tugged backward with the force of Pacific air as she stared ahead, likely searching for the sunset, as he'd been doing. It was not to be found, hidden behind the thick covering of clouds that promised a storm sometime during the night.

Rain he could handle. Hopefully, it'd be a better night than the last.

A sagging sensation Brayden wasn't sure how to define sank through him. This honeymoon hadn't begun well. He'd spent much of the night after they'd arrived at the seaside hotel rubbing Audrey's back while she threw up, or dashing out into the rain to get some ginger ale or soup. When she hadn't been perched over the bowl of the toilet, tears had seeped quietly from her eyes.

His wife had spent their first night of marriage either sick or crying. Not at any point in his life what he'd imagined for his first night as a married man. Even so, he'd tried his best to be what she'd needed. To comfort her, to assure her that their families would accept their marriage, even if the phone calls made after they'd checked into the hotel had been strained at best. Audrey had responded to his attempts with apologies.

That had made him feel worse.

He'd been sure of this course. Absolutely positive. But holding Audrey last night while she'd cried herself to sleep hadn't figured into his plans. The anxiety that literally made her sick had done what no amount of warnings or demands from either Brandon or Tim had been able to do—made Brayden wonder if this really had been the best thing.

For her. Had he really, *carefully* considered things from her side?

If Brayden avoided anything, it was fessing up to having been wrong. He didn't want to now either. But he did feel a little sick for the girl at his side. Again, he looked at his wife. Now she stood, arms tucked up against her chest, eyes shut, breathing deeply. Reaching for her hair, he fingered the wind-captive curls until her green gaze sought his face.

"Feeling sick again?" He hoped not. How much more could she throw up and still stand upright? Not to mention the baby.

Baby . . . A quick mental shove put an end to wherever that thought was going.

"No." Crimson crept up her neck, above the hoodie he'd bought her at a seaside shop earlier that afternoon, and spread to her cheeks. "I'm so sorry, Brayden. I'm sure that wasn't—"

"Stop that. Now." He turned toward her and tugged her hip until she pivoted into his arms. "I told you not to worry about it. No more worrying about any of it, okay? We're married now. It's done. There's nothing more to stew over." Cradling the back of her head, he willed her to relax against him.

As if obediently yielding, she leaned in, and then her hands lifted to skim the fabric of his pullover until they anchored on his shoulders.

"That's better," he whispered, rubbing her back. "Let's just enjoy this moment. This deserted beach. Here it's just you and me and no cares to be upset about."

No medical exams looming or family disappointments to stress over. Nothing but Audrey, soft against him, as a Pacific storm brewed over the swelling sea. It was a good moment. Not what he'd imagined for his honeymoon—he'd pictured a warm beach and a different woman. But that didn't matter now.

This was the reality he had. They had. And it'd be okay. In fact, he knew a sweet moment of real contentment. He'd married a smart, tender young woman. Could have done way worse.

He laid his cheek against her soft hair and soaked in this rare space of internal peace.

It was short lived. There, in the quiet space between him and his new wife, Brandon's phone call from last night stole that moment of rest. His brother had been positively livid. If they'd been face to face, Brayden felt certain he'd be feeling the swelling and bruises left behind by Brandon's fists.

"What the heck are you thinking?" Brandon had thundered into the phone.

Brayden had known he shouldn't have answered that call. Why had he? "Calm down, Brandon. I got just got married. It's not a crime."

Brandon was unimpressed. "I can't believe how incredibly stupid you're being. You run on flaming emotion, with little thought. You're heedless of how your actions will impact the future. Worse, you don't seem to care at all how they affect others. How can you be that entirely self-absorbed?"

"How about you climb off your podium, preacher. We got married, that's all. You act like I don't deserve to be happy or something. Are you that self-righteous?"

"Stop it, Brayden. It's about time you grow up. For Audrey's sake, you'd better do it quick. Start being the man you want everyone to believe you are."

Brayden had hung up on his brother. Wished the conversation was so easily severed in his memory.

"Brayden?" Audrey's fingers curled into the fleece at his shoulders.

Likely, she could feel his tension and would be blaming herself for it. Brandon's being a jerk wasn't Audrey's problem. "No worries, Audrey." He tightened his hold on her.

"I know, but—"

Brayden swallowed back a sigh. No more tears, please. He'd had no idea she could cry this much.

"I just w-want you to b-be happy," she managed.

That was why she was crying now?

Was he happy? Despite Brandon's pious outrage, Brayden was relieved to get the deal done. Relieved he wouldn't have to face his parents as an unmarried man when they found out Audrey was pregnant, archaic as that was. He was completely relieved to avoid the *worst of the Murphy boys* badge. And at that moment, he enjoyed the feel of her tucked against him, filling his arms.

But was he happy?

Realizing he'd not responded, and the silence was telling, he firmed his hold around her and kissed her hair. "I'm good, Audrey."

She sniffed, then pushed a half step back so that she could find his eyes. A single, fat tear welled in one corner of hers and then made a slow roll down the edge of her nose. She shook her head, then moved her hands to lay her palms flat against his chest.

"I'll make you happy, Brayden. I swear it."

Unease filtered into his chest, followed swiftly by guilt. This girl was sweet and lovely and deserved better than what he could give her of his secondhand heart. Could he be more than *relieved* with her as his wife? Could he be *happy*?

Tugging her back against him, he kissed her head again and stroked those wind-wild curls. She was warm and soft in his arms, smelling of something floral and sweet. All lovely things, and he'd be content with them. But *happy*?

She's not Leah.

He had banished that exact thought weeks ago. Should have long before that, especially since Leah was married to a soldier. That story was over, not to be added to ever again.

The problem was that all his happiness had been tied up with his high school sweetheart. He didn't know how to get it back.

Chapter Eight
(IN WHICH FACING FAMILY IS HARD)

Audrey was mortified.

Who spent their first married night throwing up and sobbing? What bride was that much of a wreck? What groom wanted that to start their forever on?

Was it retribution, God? The bitter thought wasn't so much a question but an accusation. One which she immediately regretted. God hadn't made the choices that set this mess in motion, had He?

Even so, Audrey continued to wonder, in the secret places of her heart, if He hadn't allowed that first night to be awful on purpose. With it, in that dark space of her being, a seedling of resentment sprouted.

For what remained of their weekend honeymoon, Audrey focused on the promise she'd made to Brayden while they'd stood coiled together on the beach. Determination smothered heartache and shame by degrees. Brayden was right—it was done. They were married. Didn't matter that Daddy had actually yelled at her—one of the few times he'd ever done so—or that Mom had cried when Audrey had called to let them know where she was and what she and Brayden had done. Nor did it matter, from the one side of the conversation she could hear when Brayden had called his parents, that the Murphys were not thrilled either.

She and Brayden were married now. The only way was forward from that point on. Audrey let that sink in deep during their seaside weekend, and as it did, utter resolve fortified her for life ahead. She and Brayden would be happy.

With everything she had in her, she'd find a way to make her husband glad that he'd married her.

From the moment on the beach when that decision and declaration filled her heart and left her mouth, the weekend ironed out. Thank goodness. It became almost like an actual honeymoon.

As if he was thinking the same thing, Brayden's hand left the steering wheel and sought hers as they traveled toward Audrey's hometown. With gentle warmth, he lifted it from her leg and pressed her knuckles against his lips. A swarm of happy butterflies took flight in her middle, and Audrey turned her palm so she could twine her fingers in his. "The coast was a good idea."

With a gleam in his dark eyes, he glanced at her and winked. "I told you to trust me."

"Yes. You did."

"The rest will work out as well."

It was easier to take him on faith now. "You're sure I'll get into the pre-nursing program?"

"I'm sure. You'll have some paperwork to do when we get home, but I talked to the right people. You have a spot."

Home. How bizarre and yet lovely to push her thoughts toward some other place when it came to that word. Though, picturing it, exactly, was difficult. Audrey had never been to Brayden's apartment.

"Tell me what home looks like," she said.

Eyes on the road as the car sped toward the foothills ahead, Brayden shrugged. "Just an apartment. One bedroom. Small kitchen."

"Is it a mess? Like a total bachelor's place?"

Snorting, he gave her a side glance. "Not sure how to take that."

"Are you a messy person?"

"Nope."

"Would Brandon tell me differently?"

"Brandon would tell you that I ate off the floor with filthy hands if it meant that you'd like me less."

"That's not true."

Brayden's jaw tightened, and he wriggled his fingers from their weave with hers. "Why do you care what Brandon would say?"

Audrey sat back a bit at the nip in his tone. "Only because Megan says he's the tidiest man on the planet. I just wanted to gauge what standard we're working from here."

"Oh." His mouth closed in a flat line, but the tension in his jaw loosened a touch. As an awkward silence lengthened, Brayden rubbed the side of his jaw. "I don't leave my dirty socks and underwear on the floor. And I wash dishes when the sink is too full to fill the coffeemaker. Does that give you a gauge?"

"Yes, thank you." Another beat of quiet went by. "So a little bit like Brandon."

A deep frown pulled on Brayden's mouth. "No. Nothing like Brandon."

Audrey studied her husband—the tightening of his jaw, the narrowing of his eyes as the intensity of his stare out the windshield ratcheted up. What exactly was the deal between Brayden and Brandon? Was this hot reaction to a mild comparison to his brother simply because Brandon hadn't approved of Brayden's pursuit of Audrey?

There was more to it, she was certain. After all, why would Brandon disapprove of his brother and her in the first place if there wasn't already animosity between them? Apparently mutual animosity.

Well, that didn't need to intrude upon their pursuit of happiness, did it?

Not wanting to spend the next three hours in the car in this hovering tension, Audrey reached for Brayden's hand again. When he glanced at her, she lifted a small smile, which he returned by half a measure. Wanting more than that, Audrey tucked the back of his knuckles to her cheek and then turned to press a kiss to his fingers. "I like the sound of Audrey Murphy."

"Do you?" Another glance her way, and this time, his flash of a smile nearly reached his eyes. "It has a good ring to it."

"Thank you for marrying me."

He squeezed her fingers and then brought their hands to rest together on the console between them. The car was easing into the first curve of the climb before he spoke again. "Are you going to be okay when we face your parents?"

At that, her stomach twisted. She did her best to ignore it. *It's done. We're married, no going back.* "Like you said, they'll accept it. Eventually."

"We don't have to stay there tonight, if it's too uncomfortable. We can load what you need and head to my place."

His place? What happened to *home*? "No, I think we'd better stay. I'm not anywhere close to packed, and I think we've done enough running already."

Brayden's jaw tightened again. He didn't want to stay at the Alexanders', where Audrey and her parents had been living until the new cottage could be built. "I could call Megan. Surely our news has reached her by now. We could stay with her and Brandon." Though how that would be better for Brayden, she wasn't sure. Maybe because Brayden could push back on his brother. Handling an angry father-in-law might be more of a delicate challenge.

"I guess we'll see how it goes when we get there. I'm sure to get an earful from Brandon, though."

Likely a justified earful, though she felt a new sprout of resentment against Brandon. Why was he so bossy? Perhaps she'd found the reason Brayden resented him. Just like that, Audrey decided that she was on her husband's side. After all, even Megan had said that Brandon was too hard.

Too severe. Who was more likely than Brayden to have borne the brunt of all that serious severity while they were growing up?

As they came out of another curve on the mountain highway, Brayden eased the car to a stop, guiding it to the side of the road. Audrey watched him with concern as he set it in park and stared out the windshield.

"Everything okay?"

He huffed. "Promise me you won't act ashamed." Suddenly those dark eyes were fixed on her face, intense and demanding. Quite a lot like his too-severe older brother, actually. "I can't stand that, Audrey."

Was he rebuking her for that first night? He'd been so kind and tender about it while they were on the beach.

"And don't say anything about the baby. Not yet."

Audrey scowled. He was speaking to her as if she were his child. "I'm not an idiot, Brayden." Though recent decisions seemed to indicate otherwise. She cooled her ire, hoping to extinguish his, and reached to thumb the strong line of his chin. "And I'm not ashamed to be your wife."

"No?" His eyebrows lifted, letting the harshness of his dark look diminish.

With an open palm, she covered his jaw, thumbing his lower lip. When his eyes slid shut, she leaned in to brush a soft kiss on his mouth. "Of course I'm not ashamed to be your wife."

Brayden nipped a soft kiss against her lips. "Don't ever be."

"Okay." She couldn't imagine the possibility anyway.

He looked at her, fingering the tangle of curls she'd pinned out of her face. "We're a team now, Audrey. We have to show them that."

"Okay. But this sounds like a defensive strategy meeting. Makes me think you're worried."

"A little. They were already mad that I proposed to you. This has got to have them fuming."

"Yes. But like you said, they'll get past it. It's done."

"Right. It's done."

"And it's going to be okay."

"Exactly." He pressed a kiss to her forehead. "As long as we're on the same page."

—ele—

Fuming was an apt description. Tim had set a glare on Brayden before he even exited the car after he parked in front of the great stone house belonging to the Alexanders, and he hadn't relaxed it in the two hours since. Once again Brayden mentally lined up Audrey's father with his own and found them congruent, which meant he'd be in for round two once he faced his own father.

One foe at a time though. Somehow, he needed to figure out how to flip Tim from opponent to friend. Well, *friend* might be a stretch.

In that two-hour block of time, Audrey had scarcely left Brayden's side, usually holding tightly to his hand and putting on that unified front he'd asked her for. At least there was that. She was more stiff spined to her dad than he'd hoped for, which made him grateful. Perhaps a little smug too. Nah, that secure, lifted sensation in his chest wasn't smug. It was pride, in her. Though he liked her easygoing, want-everyone-to-be-happy personality, he also appreciated discovering again that she did have a backbone. Particularly when she employed it for him.

But she couldn't cling to his hand forever. Not when she needed to pack her life to move in with him. Though even then, he'd intended to be at her side.

Into a tense silence between Tim and Shay Smith and the newly married Murphys, Audrey sighed. "This isn't changing. I realize you're upset, but the fact is, I'm married to Brayden now. I hope that you'll accept that sooner than later. In the meantime, I need to pack."

"When did you figure you'd move?"

"We'll load up tomorrow," Brayden said.

Shay's eyes, red from tears that had likely been falling since the phone call announcement on Friday, widened. "Tomorrow? That soon?"

"I have phase one medical exams in a couple of weeks. I can't afford to lose any more study time."

Tim stepped forward, fire flaring hotter in his glare. "Then why did you rush into stealing my—"

"Daddy, stop. We've done this round several times over. It's done." Audrey left Brayden's side, sliding her hand from his, and moved to stand in front of her father. "Please, Daddy. Try to be happy." Her hand gripped his arm.

Tim moved his glare from Brayden to Audrey, and the anger in his expression softened. "How can you expect that from me, Audrey? This isn't like you. Sneaking away. Breaking our hearts. How can I be happy when you've married a man who has changed you so drastically?"

Audrey flinched, and her look dropped to the floor. The arrow pierced Brayden squarely in the chest. To battle the sting of shame, he summoned a flood of fury. He began to stride toward them, but Audrey held up a staying hand.

"We all need a break from this. I'm going to pack." She looked back at her dad. "Please don't say things that will make this worse. Believe it or not, this is hard for me too. Don't make me choose, Daddy."

Sniffing and swiping at the flood of tears on her face, Shay moved toward the door, following her daughter. "I'll help."

Brayden pivoted to go with his wife. "That won't be necess—"

A firm grip fell on his shoulder and pulled him to a halt. "You *will* give her mother this."

Brayden turned back to Tim, body wound tight, but the anger waiting on the older man's face gave him pause. Tim was livid, and Brayden didn't doubt that a fist buried into his nose was a real possibility. Not something he'd have ever imagined Tim capable of until that very moment.

He swallowed. Perhaps there was a more diplomatic way to handle this situation. Audrey had begged her dad not to make her choose. Though Brayden was certain she'd chose him—she already had—he didn't want to force that position on her either.

Time to start building some bridges.

"Of course, sir." With intentional measure, Brayden relaxed his stance and cleared his throat. "Forgive me that. I just want to make sure my wife is okay."

A look of disgust morphed Tim's anger. "Your *wife*? What kind of man swoops into another man's home to steal his daughter? You are a spineless thief, Brayden Murphy. And completely without honor. You are nothing like your brother, and I am clueless why my daughter lost her head and married you. What did you do to her?"

Brayden clenched his jaw as his fingers rolled tight into fists. "I married her, that's all. I haven't stolen her from you. If you lose her, that will be your fault, not mine."

For a hot second, Tim held his glare. Then it was as though the walls toppled. He stepped backward and collapsed into a wingback chair. Shoulders slumping, he covered his head with both hands and exhaled a shuddering breath. "How could you do it, Brayden? My baby girl. My only child. Don't you know how deeply this cuts? Can't you imagine how I've struggled to see her grow up? To let her go, little bits at a time. Now, all of the sudden, without any real warning, she's gone." He looked up, agony in his eyes. "Her mom will never get to spend giddy moments planning the wedding of Audrey's dreams. I'll never get to walk her down the aisle, to give her away knowing she'll be taken care of. We're her parents, Brayden. I'm her *father*! How could you think that this was okay?"

Tim's anger was manageable. Brayden could harden himself against it. But this? The shame crowded out self-defense. Brayden looked at the tips of his shoes and then shut his eyes as the hurt in the man's voice shook him to the core Brayden typically ignored. "She'll be taken care of, Tim. I promise."

A defeated, broken man met his look. "I don't trust your promises, Brayden. There's no way around that. I can't fathom how you could expect me to."

Another dart finding a vulnerable spot in Brayden's armor. He could only nod, because how could he expect Tim to trust his word? He'd run off with the man's daughter. Though he didn't want it to, that fact sank in deep and did what likely it should. Brayden cleared his throat against the dark emotions. "Even so, I promise just the same." He edged closer, feeling worse by the moment. Like a small boy caught in a lie. A boy who now had no way out and had lost all respect. But he would have anyway, even if he'd not married her. Only more so, if possible. There was only forward now. "Audrey and me, we'll be okay. Maybe in time, you'll be okay with us too."

Tim's gaze moved away, becoming vacant and morose as he faced a large window that gave view to the gardens the man had tended for years. Suddenly Brayden visualized a savage storm tearing apart the organized and well-tended beauty of that outdoor space. Destroying the beauty. Years of work and love terrorized by an outside force.

You are that storm.

Brayden looked away. The image made him sick.

Chapter Nine

(IN WHICH THE CLOUDS BEGIN TO CLEAR)

Audrey had never ridden such highs and lows. She hadn't been prone to emotional instability before she'd met Brayden. In quiet moments, when she couldn't call sleep to hush her roiling thoughts, she wondered over the mystic spell her husband seemed to wield over her.

It was because she loved him. That was the only conclusion she could figure. Love at first sight, for no substantial reason at all.

From the moment her vision collided with his, her heart had set a new course, and the destination was Brayden Murphy. Though he looked very much like his brother Brandon—granted, a slighter build—his dark eyes set him apart immediately from that brother. Brayden's dark-brown gaze had danced with mischief and daring. His personality matched that twinkle. Brayden blew past fear and boundaries, and he laughed wildly while doing so.

Exactly her opposite, and exhilarating.

The wonder of actually being married to that man took her to new and glorious heights. He brought spunk into her world, and she crawled out of her shell-ish personality. Cleaning the tiny kitchen that was *theirs*—how amazing was that?—rearranging mismatched dishes, and reorganizing the closets that they now shared had been nothing short of delightful. Especially when those tasks had been interrupted by the man she thrilled to call *husband* emerging from his deep study to find a snack or to see what she was up to. Or to explore the wonder and benefits of marriage.

In those breathtaking moments, Brayden played the role of newlywed perfectly, causing her doubts about his love to fade. Making her believe exactly as he'd claimed all along: they'd be okay. Making her believe that she could keep her promise and make him happy.

Such highs.

Matched in equal measure by these lows that found her late at night. While Brayden enjoyed unhindered sleep, Audrey's rest was held away by persistent whispering doubts.

He's still never said the words. Did Brayden love her? Maybe not to the measure she loved him, but it seemed so.

Daddy's still so mad. It'd been nearly two weeks. Weeks of busyness for her, of setting up house and filling out applications and getting transcripts and financial aid and changing important paperwork to reflect her married status. And weeks of silence from Daddy. Would he never forgive her? She missed him. And Mom. And the Alexanders, and Megan and Brandon. Though at least Megan called her and they talked at least once a week.

Still, it seemed Audrey had given up her whole world to be with Brayden.

They'll all know the truth soon enough . . . She'd finally set up a doctor's appointment. Her first visit was in a couple of days. Should the baby be born when it was due, it'd be hard to claim that it was early, because this lying business caused the dragons of her sleep to come alive. When she finally would find rest, those nightmares from her childhood proved themselves unbanished. She knew exactly why.

Because you are a liar.

Tears couldn't be contained in those lonely moments veiled in the dark. She would let them roll quietly, when only she would know about them.

One such night, she sniffed. Brayden rolled from his back to his side. In the darkness, his fingers found her face and gently traced the trail of her tears.

"Audrey," he'd whispered, "why are you crying?"

"I'm not." More lying. It was like she'd loosed a dam and out they poured, easy as you please.

"Your face is wet." He propped up on one elbow. "Tell me why."

Audrey had to pull in a shaky breath, and even so, the words came hard. "I miss my parents."

Brayden let a space of silence lengthen long enough that she wondered if he was scowling at her. Upset with her for these tears she'd tried not to bother him with. But once again chasing the doubts about his heart for her, he'd wrapped an arm around her and pulled her close against him. "It's only been a couple of weeks. They'll come around."

Before her marriage, she'd never gone a whole day without talking to her family. Two weeks seemed like an eternity. "What did my dad say to you while Mom and I were packing?"

Sighing, Brayden kissed her head and lay back against his pillow. "Never mind."

Audrey adjusted against him. "Did he say he never wanted to see us again?"

"No. I don't think your dad is like that."

"He isn't. He never was, anyway. I barely ever got in trouble though, so maybe . . ."

Brayden chuckled. "I can imagine you as the perfect child."

With a palm against his chest, she sat up. "I didn't say that."

"No, but I can imagine it."

"Do you think I'm uptight?"

Again, he chuckled. "No." His fingers pushed into her hair, and he eased her back down against him. "I think you've not slept well in weeks. I think that this is the first truly rebellious thing you've ever done in your life. And I think you're emotional right now." He moved to kiss her mouth before she could protest that patronizing statement. "And I think your parents will come around. They love you."

"Have yours come around?"

"My mom says she expects me to bring you home soon."

"Is that a good thing?"

"Yes, it's a good thing."

"What about your dad?"

Another soft kiss landed at her hairline. "Go to sleep, Audrey. Time will work all of it out, and we'll be okay."

A new sprout of irritation germinated, and this one was with him. This was a real crisis in her world. She was allowed to cry over it, and Brayden couldn't just tell her to go to sleep! As if that would sweep all of her heartache away and everything would be fine in the morning. She fisted the covers near her hand and worked to stifle that annoyance. He was just trying to encourage her, to be a good husband.

"How do you think you did on your test?" Though she was winning the battle against her ire, she also still couldn't sleep. Since he was obviously awake too, they might as well talk.

"I don't know. I guess I'll find out when the results are published."

"Two weeks?"

"That's what they said."

She blew out an exasperated sigh. "That's a long time to wait."

"I'll bet the month of December about kills you then, doesn't it?"

"As a matter of fact, it does. The advent calendar helps though. And Mom has a yearly baking calendar that she follows in December, so that marks time too."

"Do you get to do the pies?" In the short time as husband and wife, Brayden had seen Audrey's affection for pie—and had also delighted in the discovery that she not only loved eating them but baking them too.

His comment drew a soft chuckle, and she smiled as she lay her cheek against him. "Yes."

"Is it going to be awful waiting for this baby to come?"

Audrey froze, holding her breath.

"What's wrong?" he asked when her stiff silence drew out.

Her heart throbbed warmly. "You haven't talked about the baby since you proposed."

"Neither have you."

She thought on that. No, she hadn't talked about the baby. It'd seemed like an unspoken contract between them to not bring it up. "I guess not."

"Are you scared?"

Yes. Yes, she was terrified, for many reasons. She hadn't planned on being a mom at nineteen and wasn't sure she was ready for it. How did one even do it? What would she do if the baby cried all night? How would she ever become a nurse with an infant to care for? And Brayden—he'd not said a word about it. She had no idea how he felt about becoming a father so soon. Truthfully, she wasn't any more certain that he'd be a good dad than she was sure she'd be a decent mom. Fact was, they both had some growing up to do, and Audrey knew it. Would they be ready when this baby arrived?

All she knew was that Brayden didn't want anyone to know that she'd gotten pregnant before they were married. No, that wasn't all she knew. She knew he wouldn't have married her if not for the baby.

Sadness engulfed her heart, taking her to a new low that very nearly canceled all the highs of previous days. A fresh crop of tears seeped from her eyes.

"Aw, Audrey." Brayden rubbed her shoulder. "We'll figure it all out."

She nodded, willing to let him think her tears were about the fear of becoming a mom. Almost anything was better than saying the truth out loud: that she cried because she knew he hadn't wanted to marry her. She wasn't his first choice for his wife. Sniffing, she swiped at the tears before they soaked his shirt. "How do you know we'll figure it out?"

"Everyone does."

"Not everyone. There are some bad parents out there."

"Not you." He wrapped her in a tighter hug. "If anyone is going to be a good mom, it's you."

"I think you're required to say that to your wife."

"Nah. I really believe it. You're smart and hardworking and borderline too sweet."

"Borderline too sweet?"

He laughed. "Yes. But only just toeing the line. You do have some fire in you, I'm happy to say."

"You didn't think I did?"

"Hmm . . ." Brayden rolled to his side, adjusting his hold around her. "You surprise me. You keep surprising me. In good ways."

"Oh."

"Now go to sleep."

"You're bossy." She almost added *like Brandon*. But she bit back the last part.

"They teach you that in medical school. It's part of the curriculum."

"Hmm. I don't think they mean for you to use it at home."

"See, this little bit of sass. That's what I'm talking about. Surprising."

"In a good way?"

"Well, at the moment, maybe not so much. But"—he leaned back to look down at her, though it was really too dark to make out his expression—"on the whole, I like the girl I married."

"And that surprises you?"

Brayden tucked her into his shoulder and kissed her hair. "Go to sleep, Audrey. That's almost-a-doctor's orders."

Audrey stilled against him, wavering between delight and disappointment. It was good he liked the wife he had. Sad that the fact surprised him. Sad and revealing.

Disappointment won. But she squeezed back the tears until they no longer threatened and tried her best to do as the almost-a-doctor holding her said.

ele

Brayden turned the key to his apartment slowly and then eased the door open as quietly as he could. Though he'd been up for six hours, working as part of the grounds crew for a prestigious golf course since four in the morning, he hoped Audrey had taken his encouragement to sleep in. Sometimes she did. In the month since he'd married her, she'd struggled with sleep. Much, if not all, of that issue could be attributed to the seismic shifting of her world over the past many weeks.

Even so, Brayden looked forward to the time she'd settle into this new life. She worried so much. Quite often, when she thought he was asleep, she would cry. He didn't like that at all. This marriage was supposed to solve problems, not make new ones.

For him, having Audrey with him, being his wife, had solved much of his anxiety. He'd been able to focus on his studying, rather than worrying about her and how she was handling their secret crisis a few hours away. And enjoying all the privileges of married life . . . well, that hadn't hurt anything. If asked, Brayden could honestly say adjusting to their marriage hadn't been much of a struggle at all.

But he didn't like that his wife cried when she didn't think he could hear her. Sleep, he suspected, would be the most effective cure to that problem. Audrey was flat-out exhausted. Pregnant women, his studies informed him, usually were so anyway. A pregnant woman who couldn't sleep for worry over her family's disappointment in her was bound to crash, and crash hard.

This marriage was supposed to ease both their burdens.

Brayden crept into the apartment, quietly closing the door behind him, and stopped a few steps inside to remove the grass-stained shoes he wore to work. He tucked his headlamp into the ball cap that read *Hillside Green Country Club* in embroidered gold letters and set them both on top of his work sneakers. Next, he tugged off the hoodie that smelled of mower and gas-powered hedge trimmer, both of which he'd used on the back nine.

He snuck into the kitchen, to the closet that housed ductwork and the stacked washer/dryer combo. The hoodie went into the washing tub, and then he slipped off his damp socks, dropping them in as well. He tugged his T-shirt free from the waistline of his jeans and pulled it over his head.

A pair of hands slipped around his bare waist from behind, causing him to suck in a sharp breath at the thrill of her touch. He freed himself of the soiled shirt and dropped it in with the hoodie and socks, then pivoted in Audrey's arms.

"I hoped you'd still be asleep." He settled a loose hold around her and pressed a kiss to her brow. "Did I wake you?"

"No. The mail came a while ago."

Brayden frowned. If the slight click of the mail slot closing had woken her, that wasn't a good sign. "You didn't sleep well again."

She shrugged and then pressed her face against his chest.

"I need a shower. I'm sure I stink."

She answered with a long, exaggerated inhale, and then looked up at him with a smile. "You trimmed hedges this morning, didn't you?"

"Yep. And mowed greens." He winked. "The usual."

"I don't know how you get up so early to work."

"I sleep at night."

Audrey's mouth twisted, and she tried to give him a stink-eye. Her attempt was thwarted by a grin she couldn't hold back.

"What are you hiding, Mrs. Murphy?"

"A letter came for you today." She leaned back in his arms.

Brayden looked at his wife. Her strawberry-blond curls held a morning fuzz she typically didn't allow others to see. If she didn't use cream to tame them into order, she would straighten them. He preferred this wild, unmanaged look on her—something he got all to himself. He also preferred the way her green eyes gleamed with excitement, as they did just then. And speaking of preferences, Audrey's creamy skin, silk to his touch, was currently covered with nothing more than a T-shirt she'd stolen from his drawer the night before.

Yep. He sure liked being married. He pulled her back against him and dipped to nuzzle her neck. "Did you snoop into my mail?"

"Yes. I did."

He kissed the exposed skin at her collarbone where the loose shirt slipped. "And?" She shivered in his arms, and he dipped for another taste.

"Good news." Her words came breathless.

Brayden straightened to look at her, not missing the way her pulse leapt in her neck. Gooseflesh rippled over his body at the feel of her fingertips swirling against his shoulder, then his back, before she settled a hold at the base of his neck. Man, his wife could make him feel good. She could tell him that he'd gotten kicked out of medical school in that moment, and he might not care. Lost in the headiness of her touch, and the promise of pleasures nearby, Brayden bent to find her lips with his own.

She slipped her hands from the back of his neck to press both palms on his chest, stalling the kiss. "You're not going to ask?"

"Not sure whatever is in some letter could beat what I've got in front of me right now."

As her smile bloomed full, a warm blush filled her cheeks. And the look that flooded those lovely green eyes—warm, intense—it gripped his middle and shook him to his core.

His wife adored him.

What man alive didn't want that? But in the midst of that security there was something wholly terrifying. For weeks Brayden had done his best to ignore that—the thing that rattled him so deeply. He wanted only the euphoria that came with these intimate moments. Not the counterweight of whatever was gripping him in the middle and demanding more than he had.

Audrey's gaze didn't waver from his eyes, though Brayden had let his wander because the intensity flaring within him was too much.

"You passed," she whispered.

He focused on the news. A good enough distraction from what he could only identify as inadequacy. "I passed? It was from the medical board?"

She bit her bottom lip, and her expression turned proud. "You passed. I knew you would." Both hands left his chest and framed the planes of his jaw, and then she pulled him back in to finish that stalled kiss.

He passed. That was a relief. And this . . . Audrey's reward for his efforts? Hmm.

Brayden took what she gave, which was everything. Though she'd struggled with the transition of this marriage, made more difficult because of her parents' disapproval and her missing her best friend, Audrey never held back from him.

Later, when he fingered the softness of those unkept curls as she nodded off into the rest she'd so desperately needed, that empty, ugly feeling rushed back into the space that had been temporarily filled with the pleasure she'd given him. It came with such strength, Brayden was forced to examine what it was and why it kept invading.

She deserves more.

Three words defined the void. Pushing off their bed and aiming for the shower, Brayden chose not to acknowledge the implication.

Chapter Ten

(IN WHICH THE HONEYMOON IS OVER)

Beneath a warm late-summer sun, in between classes that had resumed two days before, Brayden stopped short in the middle of the parade grounds on campus. His heart froze as he studied the profile of the woman who, at a mere glimpse, had demanded his attention from across the green. Blond hair, shining golden in the bright sun, her petite stature and profile were as familiar to him as his own reflection. If she turned to look at him, Brayden was certain he'd find the ocean-blue eyes he'd not long before thought to drown in for the rest of his life.

Leah.

Was that woman across the wide space of manicured lawn truly her? He had no reason to conjure her up. Honestly, he hadn't thought about his ex-girlfriend in months. Not since he'd married Audrey. And that'd been a relief, like the long-overdue healing of a gaping wound. He squinted and scowled. Surely it wasn't her—she hadn't any reason to be there.

As if sensing his focused study, the woman turned and locked eyes with him.

A pain squeezed in his chest. "Leah." He breathed her name as if it was sacred. Or, perhaps as if it was unsafe. A curse that set his footing on treacherous ground.

As she held his gaze, her countenance lifted into a smile shared only between them, summoning a skip in his pulse and a slow grin to his mouth.

Treacherous indeed. As Leah's smile brightened, she turned her body toward him. It was her!

It was her. Lips closing, he felt a scowl tugging on his brow again.

Why was she there?

Brayden had heard she was going to school somewhere on the southern coast, close to where her husband was stationed. Far away from Brayden, from all the plans they'd made together.

Her husband.

The two words tugged reality back to mind. She should *not* be there, and he should not be having this havoc-in-his-heart sort of response. In tandem with his thoughts, as if to reinforce his place, Leah placed a hand over her belly, the swell beneath her palm an unmistakable proclamation. She was married and was pregnant.

A bolt, hot and liquid, surged through his chest, as if this revelation was shocking. It shouldn't have been. He'd known exactly why Leah had broken things off with him—to marry another man. More to the point, *he* was married. *His* wife, who adored him, was pregnant. Seeing his ex-girlfriend like this shouldn't provoke this sort of reaction.

Brayden shored up his smile and forced stiff strides toward Leah, who waited for his approach. When he was within two strides, she reached to hug him. A sense of disbelief, followed quickly with warning, buzzed loud and strong in his head, but he returned her hug with a rigid arm around her shoulders.

"Brayden." His name was a breath of airy relief from her lips, ruffling to life things deep within that should have been long-since dead. "I was hoping to run into you."

"You were?" He stepped back, forcing her hands to fall away from him, and sealed his lips as he forced indifference into his expression. She merely smiled under his study—a disarming talent she had often employed in moments of tension. "I'm shocked to run into you. What are you doing here?"

Her hand stroked her belly as she lifted a one-shoulder shrug. "Aiden is deployed for at least six months. I didn't want to be alone and pregnant so far from home, so I transferred."

A fresh glower pinched his brow. "We're two hours from home here," Brayden said flatly.

"Two is much less than six." Leah tipped her head and looked at him, as if not understanding why he wasn't as happy to see her as she was to see him. "Besides, I knew I'd have at least one friend here." She reached for his arm and squeezed his elbow. "Just like old times."

Brayden moved from her touch. Friends? Could he and Leah be *friends*? She'd broken promises, ripped out his heart, and flung it back to him as if it were nothing more than a ball cap stolen from his head. He'd framed his future and dreams with her in his mind. She'd been everything to him, but he'd been disposable to her. Now she was there, married to another man and pregnant with that stranger's child, and expected Brayden's friendship?

Absolutely *not* like old times.

You're married now too. The calm voice of reason spoke into his building rant.

There was that. But his marriage wasn't an utter betrayal.

No, just a cover-up.

"Brayden?" Leah edged nearer and laid her hand against his arm again. "Everything okay?"

He looked at the fingers resting on his arm. As if they belonged there, like she had a right to touch him. A diamond glared back at him, certainly one that was much more valuable than the cubic zirconia he'd hastily purchased and had given to Audrey. A concoction of guilt and anger zipped through his veins. This time, he jerked his arm from her hand.

"I'm fine." He jammed both hands into his pockets. "I've got class though. Infectious diseases." Jerking a nod toward the building where he'd attend his next class, he sidestepped Leah. "Better go."

"Wait."

Now past her, he pivoted to face her. "For what, Leah?" He didn't even try to disguise the edge in his tone.

Her lovely blue eyes filled with hurt as her expression folded. "Brayden, I chose to enroll in the PA course here on purpose. I need a friend. I thought—"

Physician assistant. Great. They'd have classes together, then. Brayden shook his head. "Leah, I think our history is going to make that a little hard."

"Does it have to?" She closed the space between them again, her steady, open gaze somehow hypnotic.

How could it not? Brayden's mind whirled with the contradiction of what seemed simple to her being impossible to him.

"You still care about me, right?"

Swallowing, he battled a torch of heat that flared in his chest. Did she have any right to ask such things? "I have to go."

"Brayden." Now the clip in her voice was firm. "We're adults. We can leave childish things behind us."

Was it childish to believe he couldn't be friends with a woman who had wrecked his heart? Was it childish to believe trying it would be a disaster? And what of his wife? Brayden blew out a slow breath, then shifted his distant stare from some unfocused point on the green back to Leah. "I'm married, Leah."

Her mouth tightened for a moment, and then she shrugged. "That makes two of us, then. There's nothing to worry about. Nothing to lose." Those eyes held his, the emotion in them shifting from confident to pleading. "Please, Bray. I really need a friend right now."

Nothing to lose? There was more at stake here than Leah and himself. So much more. But then again, there was no going back to what used to be, was there? He and Leah were both grown-ups now, not the emotional and foolish kids they'd once been. They each wore a ring on their left hand, as a solid reminder of where they belonged. Friendship might be possible.

Might didn't seem like a good gamble.

Uncertainty remained fixed in his head. Brayden rubbed his jaw, determined to tell Leah it wasn't a good idea. Instead, he found himself nodding.

Leah brightened, her smile triumphant. He should have expected nothing less. She'd always been an expert at getting what she wanted, and delighted at her victories. Once again, her hand was on his arm. "I knew I could count on you. You've never let me down yet." After a pivot on her toes, she nearly skipped away.

Victorious.

A pit yawned in Brayden's gut as his thoughts moved toward Audrey, who was at that moment in class somewhere on the other side of campus. What would she think of Leah being there? Of Leah telling Brayden she needed him to be her friend? Of Leah's victory over him?

Brayden could picture the innocent adoration in Audrey's green eyes, and he could imagine the light that now upheld his confidence dimming. The hole in his middle widened further.

He couldn't tell his wife about Leah resurfacing in his world. Somehow he'd have to figure out how to push Leah away without Audrey ever knowing about her.

⸺ele⸺

Audrey blinked her heavy eyelids open at the sound of the door clicking open and then shut. A heavy sigh escaped her body as she sat up, pushing off her face the mass of curls that had fallen over her eyes. She hadn't meant to actually fall asleep, just sit and rest her weary eyes for a minute before she started supper. If Brayden was home, that meant she'd dozed off for close to an hour.

The man wandered around the narrow wall that separated the doorway from the rest of the apartment, shoulders slumped. He'd removed his shoes at the door—a habit he'd acquired from working wicked-early mornings as a groundskeeper at the golf course—and rubbed his neck, as if it was sore.

"Long day?" Audrey spoke through a yawn that snuck up on her.

That profile of dark hair and equally dark two-day shadow turned, and Brayden's coffee-colored gaze landed on her. There was something in that look. Audrey wasn't sure exactly what it was, other than wariness, but as he held it on her for a breath, unease took firm root in her heart.

Something had happened.

Distinctly aware by now of the life growing in her middle, stretching her taught abdomen, though not nearly as much as she'd assumed at nearly six months pregnant, Audrey used the arm of the sofa to aid her as she stood. "What's wrong, Bray?"

His brows flickered. A flinch? Again, he rubbed his neck, and then his palm grazed the line of his jaw. "Nothing. Long day, as you said."

Studying his closed-off expression, Audrey wandered near enough to touch him. As she approached, Brayden dropped his look to the floor.

This was new from her husband. Brayden was confident and purposeful. Some might say arrogant, though Audrey didn't think that was true. He simply knew where he was in life and knew where he wanted to go. And went after the things he wanted. This reserve—she wasn't sure how to file it. Especially when he wouldn't look at her in the eye.

"Anything happen?" She reached to rest a palm on his shirt, her touch tentative.

The bob of his throat in a visible swallow was subtle, but Audrey caught it. As she did, the silent inhale of a long breath moved the chest beneath her hand. When Brayden redirected his focus back to her, there was a shield in his eyes.

"Nothing big." With a hand to her lower back, he pulled her close and then wrapped a hold on her. "Nothing worth talking about." He planted a kiss at her hairline. "Is supper going?"

"No, I'm sorry." She leaned back, searching for his face, feeling pushed away by this closed-off version of her new husband even as he held her against him. "I came home with plans to start chicken fajitas, but sat down to rest my eyes for a sec."

The shadow of a smile he gave her seemed a mask. "No big deal. I can make it."

"No, I'm fine. I didn't mean to fall asleep."

"Rest is good." His arms fell away, and he moved toward the kitchen. "How were your classes today?"

Audrey trailed him, latching on to the uptick in his tone. Maybe she'd imagined more there than actually was. Perhaps it was as Brayden said, just a long day. She'd actually had one too. "I might be in over my head."

Opening the fridge, Brayden didn't even glance back at her. "Nah. You'll find your stride."

"This program is pretty demanding." She took the peppers from his grasp so he could grab the chicken. "And I wasn't prepared for how tired I'd be all the time."

"You're sleeping better though, right?"

"Yes."

"And you talked to your parents last night."

That lightened her mood, sloughing worry away. "Yes."

"That makes a solid month of good conversation at least once a week, right?"

"It does."

Brayden set the pan on the glass-top stove, flicked the burner to medium, and then glanced at her with a tight grin.

It was tight. Audrey was sure of it. The corners of his eyes pinched, and not the way they did when he laughed.

"Bray, is there something—"

"Audrey, I told you, it was just a long day. Stop pestering me about it." Those dark eyes stabbed as he glared at her.

She shrank back against the counter and bit her lip. Several throbbing heartbeats of silence pulsed between them, the only sounds in the kitchen that of seasoned chicken breasts hitting hot oil in the pan. Brayden pivoted from the stove, walked to the sink, washed his hands, and then moved in front of her. She saw only the gray of his socks as she stared at the floor.

With two fingers, Brayden nudged her chin up. A repentant look held her as she lifted her gaze back to his face.

"I'm sorry," he murmured.

She raked her top teeth over her bottom lip. The pad of his thumb traced her chin, and then he cupped her face.

"Please forgive me, Audrey. I shouldn't have snapped at you."

"Of course," she whispered.

He leaned to capture her mouth in a soft kiss and then moved away, turning back to the browning chicken. Audrey pulled in a shuddered breath, unsure why she'd reacted as if he'd done something terrible. He hadn't. Everyone snapped a little sometimes. Especially when they were tired—and Brayden was.

Their summer of bliss, more or less, had come to an abrupt halt with the reconvening of classes.

He never complained, but Brayden was still working at the country club, getting up before four and working as long as he could before he needed to come home, grab a quick shower, and go to class. Like her, he was carrying a full load of challenging courses. Where there had been space at night for movies and relaxing, baking pies, or long, passionate kisses, their evenings were now spent in quiet study, her curled into one corner of the sofa with a textbook, and him on the other side, with the small comfort of an occasional brush of their fingers.

The honeymoon was over. Perhaps that was all this was. Even so, Audrey felt keenly Brayden pulling away, hiding something from her, and she didn't like it.

There was nothing for it though. Turning to face the counter, she reached for a cutting mat and began julienning the bell peppers. Next, she would slice sweet onions and quarter the lime she'd already washed before her nap. Along with the pineapple she'd cut up the day before, supper would come together quick. Perhaps Brayden would open up over their meal shared at the bar-height table he'd inherited from Connor, an older brother Audrey had only met once, at Brandon and Megan's wedding the previous fall.

As she glanced at that hand-me-down, she pushed her thoughts back to family. Things were so much better with her parents. And Brayden seemed less edgy about his brothers, less concerned with living up to some impressive, impossible standard Audrey was sure had been created in Brayden's mind and not by the other Murphy men.

Family seemed like a positive topic between them lately. "Have you heard from your parents the past couple of days?" She reached around him with the cutting mat in hand and scraped the cut peppers and onions into the pan, inhaling the aroma that made her stomach growl.

"My mom texts me every other day or so. I imagine she does all of us." Brayden fell back into easy, casual conversation. He glanced at her and dropped a quick wink. "She still asks when I'm going to bring my new wife home."

Audrey set down the paring knife and mat and let her fingers spread over the growing volleyball of her belly. "At this rate, by the time you do, you won't only be bringing home a new wife."

Rather than chuckling, as she'd hoped, Brayden's smile tightened again, and he faced the cooking food, a frown pulling the corners of his mouth down.

That did it. What was with him? Audrey went from confused and hurt by her husband's cut-off attitude to angry. "They will find out, you know. This isn't something we can hide forever."

Using a wooden spoon, Brayden rubbed the meat and vegetables across the sizzling oil.

Audrey did not appreciate being ignored. "Were you thinking we'd wait and invite them to this baby's first birthday?"

He smacked the spoon onto the counter. "I was thinking that, as already discussed, this has been a long day, and maybe it would be nice if you didn't bring up stuff that is going to cause problems."

Why would talking about their baby cause problems? "I married you so that this wouldn't be a problem. Why are we still not telling our families that there's a baby coming in the near future?"

"I'm not ready yet." He dropped every word in a low tone that acted as a punctuation on the subject. Discussion closed.

Nope. Not for her. Audrey planted her hands on her hips. "Of course, that should be a good enough reason, shouldn't it? Since we do everything according to what you want."

Arms crossed and posture nearly predatory, Brayden turned to glower at her. "What does that mean?"

"How did we get married Brayden? Did it ever occur to you that I might want my family and my best friend at my wedding? Or, you know, to actually *have* a wedding?" The vent in her anger had cracked, and now the steam rolled freely. Back straight, she tipped her chin up and stepped nearer. "Who picked the date? The town and hotel for our honeymoon? When we would move?"

"You liked the seaside."

"That's not the point! You don't think I have a voice in anything. I don't get a say. You even decided where I would go to school. Everything we do is about what is convenient for you!"

"Convenient? Really, Audrey? Do you think it's convenient to acquire a wife *and* a baby in the middle of medical school? Do you think it's convenient for me to put in fifteen-hour days so I can finish med school while figuring out how to support a nearly instant family?"

"You should have thought about that before you got me pregnant!"

Brayden's head snapped back as if she'd slapped him. Anger billowed from him like heat waves off desert sand on a July afternoon. His jaw clenched and unclenched, and his brow folded into the fiercest scowl she'd ever seen. But he said nothing.

Nothing. Just scalding, bitter silence.

Brayden reached for the stove, flicked off the burner, then rotated toward the door. More silence as he jammed one foot and then the other into his shoes. And silence as he jerked open the door and passed through it.

Click.

The door shut behind him. Leaving Audrey in the wake of Brayden's scorching silence.

Body quaking, Audrey gripped her shoulders as a sickening sensation pressed in her gut. What had she done?

Chapter Eleven

(IN WHICH HARD WORDS ARE SPOKEN)

Brayden leaned heavily back against the driver's seat in his sedan while a stiff late-summer wind rocked the parked vehicle. The parking-lot lamp flickered on three spaces to his left, immediately drawing the bugs that were determined to make the most of what was left in life before frost. Staring at the building swarm of moths, mosquitoes, and other winged nuisances, Brayden wondered what his life would look like after frost.

Everything had changed so fast. How was that possible? How had he gone from single, and rather reckless in that state, to married and nearly a dad in six short months? Up until that moment, the weight of it all hadn't really bothered him. No, what had nagged at him more than anything was not wanting his parents and brothers to find out the outcome of his reckless behavior. The actual responsibility of that outcome?

His stare shifted from the yellow-white glow of the light to the fourth window from the right, third story. No light shone there—it'd flicked off twenty minutes before. Audrey must have gone to bed.

It'd been over two hours since he'd shoved his feet into his shoes and left. In that time, he'd simply sat there. He'd fought hard against the urge to drive to a bar and let the burn of something stout and numbing drown the frustrations of his day. The fact that he was still there, parked in his assigned spot at the apartment, was a win.

Why had Audrey gotten so upset with him? He hadn't known she was mad about how they'd gotten married. Hadn't known she was upset about him arranging things so she could go into the pre-nursing program on the same campus where he was enrolled as a medical student. Why had she suddenly gathered all that and flung it at him like he was a dartboard? Hadn't they been talking about the baby? Couldn't she simply discuss the situation with him rationally?

Perhaps he'd been the irrational one. Audrey did have a point about telling their families about the baby. He'd have to make an announcement sooner rather than later. But right now, while they were away, finding their own footing without the abundance of input from his large family and the heavy involvement of hers, it seemed easier to keep it to themselves. For just a little longer. His world could be semi-normal for a few more weeks.

You should have thought about that before you got me pregnant!

Audrey's final dart, which had landed dead center, surged through his mind. Brayden sat up, wrapped both hands on the steering wheel, and gripped it with all his might. The weight of his choices over the past year pressed down hard and forced him to look at the choices he was making right then.

This whole night had been on him. Audrey had known he was off the moment he'd walked through the door. As unnerving as it was to realize that there was a person in this world who could read him that easily, he found himself attaching to her more for it. Which made the biggest frustration of his day that much worse.

Leah's reemerging into his life rocked him hard, and he didn't know what to do with that. Not any more than he knew what to do with *her*.

Would he allow the friendship Leah had asked for? How could he do that when he couldn't bring himself to tell his wife about it? How could he even think of it when his wife saw plainly that he'd been undone with one single encounter, and his trying to hide it from her had thoroughly sabotaged their night?

Life is a series of choices . . .

A line often spoken in the Murphy home.

We have to live with ripples of consequences. Be sure you can, before you toss the stone into the water.

He could live with being married to Audrey. Truthfully, as the days and weeks had gone by over the summer, he'd discovered that being her husband wasn't a bad gig at all. No one adored him the way Audrey did. No one had ever made him feel as wanted and cherished as his wife did. She loved him, and she made no secret of it. While for a time, that had merely fed his ego, now . . .

Now her love was quickly becoming the substance that sustained every part of him. He never wanted to lose it.

Which brought him back to the problem of Leah.

He should have turned and walked away the moment their eyes connected, as he would have a stranger who had never meant anything to him. Why hadn't he?

Why couldn't he?

He should.

He *would.*

Looking from his clenched hands on the steering wheel back to the darkened window that belonged to the bedroom he shared with his wife, resolution shifted his heart and mind back into alignment. Audrey was in there, likely huddled beneath the brown-and-teal quilt she'd picked out at a seaside shop while on their honeymoon. Perhaps she was crying even now. A pain jolted through his chest as he imagined her curled up, alone on their bed, quiet tears seeping onto their sheets. He didn't want that for her. He wanted her smiles and joy. And her love.

Leah could see to her own problems. Brayden had his to fix.

With a fortifying breath, he sat forward, popped the car door open, and planted his feet onto the pavement. A cool wind brushed his face, bringing a hint of sweet rain to his senses. He strode into the darkness toward the door that would lead him back home.

—*eee*—

Though she was ever tired, Audrey wavered in and out of a fitful sleep. Strange how she'd slept alone for nineteen years, but after mere months of married life, she found Brayden's absence disruptive. The empty space beside her made her lonely and anxious.

For nearly an hour after he'd left their home angry with her, Audrey had thought and prayed. She replayed the whole scene in her mind, from the moment he'd come home to that horrible one when he'd gone back out the door. There was still something going on with him that she couldn't put her finger on. Something he wasn't telling her. But even so, she'd been ugly to him, and she'd spent some time confessing that to God.

Confessing a lot of things, actually. About how she wanted this to be easy. Uncomplicated. That she didn't want to lose her parents' respect any more than she already had—and any more than Brayden wanted to lose his family's—and that made it easy to keep up this pretense. That was pride, plain and simple. While she couldn't do anything about the issue on Brayden's part, she certainly could own her own. And the ugly things she'd thrown at her husband?

Also pride.

After pouring her heart out to heaven, Brayden still hadn't returned. Audrey had no idea where he was or when he'd come back. She hoped he hadn't landed at a bar. Though certain he had his phone with him, she opted to let him be. Time to cool down, to think straight was allowed. She needed it just as much. She had put away the untouched food, washed the dishes, and changed for bed. As the world had darkened outside, she'd turned off the lights, left the front door unlocked, and crawled under the covers.

Tomorrow would be a new day. One to, she hoped, begin anew. And so she shut her eyes and willed sleep to claim her. It must have done so, even if with only limited effectiveness, because the moving of the covers and the shifting of the mattress took her from an unrestful unawareness to murky consciousness.

"Brayden?" she rasped into the darkness.

The bed shifted again, and then the light touch of his fingers warmed her shoulder. "Shh. Yeah, it's me."

"I wasn't sure you'd come—" Her words cut off as emotion stole them from her throat.

"I'm here." The heat of his body hovered over her as he leaned to kiss her temple. "I'm sorry I made you worry."

"I thought, I mean I hoped you weren't somewhere half . . ."

"Drunk?"

Audrey swallowed, partly with relief because his tone didn't bite with defense, as she'd feared. "Yes." It had been a reasonable worry though. Brayden had lost sobriety more than once since she'd known him.

"I didn't leave the parking lot."

"You didn't?"

"I've watched one of my brothers land himself in rehab for drug addiction. For a while, he lost everything. That's not a direction I want to go, especially now."

She breathed a shuddered sigh. "Oh, Bray . . ."

With the pad of his thumb, he traced her brow. "You left the door unlocked, hon. That's not safe."

"I didn't want to lock you out."

He chuckled softly. "I have a key."

The fog muddling her mind cleared. "Of course." Rolling to her back, she searched the shadowy lines of his face. By his soft tone, and that low chuckle, he'd worked through his anger. A good thing. Even better, he hadn't used a bottle to do it. She'd underestimated him. Lifting her hand, she covered the back of his as he fingered the edge of her hair. "I'm glad you came back."

The lowering of his head was slow, purposeful. As if he was asking permission, rather than assuming. Audrey reached for his head, burying her fingers into the thickness of his hair, and his lips found hers. Lingered. Then he pulled back. "You're not an inconvenience, Audrey. I'm glad to have you. And the baby . . ."

He didn't finish his thought, but as he shifted to lean on one elbow, he moved his other hand to span the swell of her belly, where their child grew. Not something Brayden did much. Had he ever, except when she'd prompted him to feel the little one squiggle within her womb? No, she thought not. He rarely acknowledged this child they'd made, a fact that she kept hidden in a sore place in her heart.

She'd thought he ignored their child because he resented the facts of their reality. Maybe even her—that he'd felt forced to take her as his wife. *Inconvenienced*. But was there a different reason? Or perhaps the baby simply wasn't the predominant thought in his mind, as it was in hers?

He caressed the small bulge of her belly and then moved again, this time to press a kiss against the spot where their baby grew. Audrey sucked in a breath as a painful delight squeezed her heart.

"Hi, little one. Daddy here."

The life within her womb moved, the sensation a rolling sort. Audrey smiled in the darkness as she lay her hand over Brayden's.

"You're not an inconvenience either. I'm sorry I said those things to your mother." The profile of his face turned, and Audrey felt his gaze on her. "I'm sorry, Audrey."

With her palm against the rough whiskers covering his cheek, Audrey guided his face back to hers and moved to capture his lips again. "Me too."

The warm breath of his sigh scattered over her face, and then his arm surrounded her, tucking her close.

"Bray?"

"Hmm?"

"What I said before you left—"

"Apology accepted, Audrey. We're done with it." He lowered her to the mattress, pressed a kiss on her forehead, and then lay down beside her.

Audrey shifted to her side and propped up on an arm. "I need to say this. What I said about you getting me pregnant . . . That was wrong, and a horrible thing for me to say. It wasn't all you. I made choices too."

In the shadows, she could see his head roll so that his eyes no longer searched her face. An uneasy silence lengthened. Brayden breathed a long sigh. "I knew how far was too far."

"So did I." She covered the place where his heart beat, and he looked back at her. "I know we made mistakes, Bray. Both of us made them. But the thing is, I don't want to see this baby as a mistake."

"Do you?"

"No. But I'm afraid you do. That you always will, and that's why you don't want to tell anyone."

Brayden rolled to his side, his hand on her hip gently guiding her to her back again, and for the second time, he covered her womb with his palm. "I'll love this little one." He spoke with firm conviction. "I already do."

She ran her hand up his arm until she came to his shoulder. "Then we'll be okay." In the dark quietness that stretched between them, peaceful and much more comfortable than it had been earlier that evening, a familiar longing ached through her.

They would be okay. This was okay, the way they were. But oh, how Audrey longed for more than okay. A void carved in her heart, yearning to be filled by his love for her.

But for that night, he was home with her, and he loved their baby. And they'd be okay. That would have to be enough.

Chapter Twelve

(IN WHICH EVERYTHING IS GOING TO BE OKAY)

Operating on three hours of sleep was no picnic. Sitting on the cool concrete of a sidewalk in the shade of a brick building, Brayden sucked down an energy drink—the second of the day—against his knowledge that the high dose of caffeine and ephedrine might get him through the day, but he'd crash hard. Medically speaking, liquid energy was not an ideal solution. Practically speaking, he was up against a wall, so to speak.

He tipped his head back, resting heavily against the three-story building that served as the medical lab, and shut his eyes. The pulse throbbing through his veins sped up as his quick pick-me-up took effect, and a buzz tingled at the back of his head. He couldn't let this become a habit.

With forefinger and thumb, Brayden rubbed the skin above his eyebrows as his thoughts took him back to the night before. He'd known couples fought. Had witnessed that truth from his own parents. Godly, loving people that they were, even so he'd witnessed some doozies between his dad and mom. Still, the echo of Audrey's outburst the night before stung. It had been as if she hadn't appreciated that all he'd done had been to make things right. To do right by her.

Did she really think that he wouldn't love his own child? Was that the meager height of her opinion of him? Surely it couldn't be. Audrey left him with no doubt of her love for him. Her admiration of him. Or maybe that esteem was directed toward the man she'd hoped he'd be. More like Brandon. Could it be that she clung to illusions he was sure to disappoint?

With a low growl, Brayden bumped his head on the brick wall behind him. This line of thinking was useless. He might as well be a dog chasing its tail for all the good it was doing him. The fight was done with. They'd made up. They'd be okay. He didn't need to waste the precious little energy he had ruminating on any of it.

"This is a strange place to sit." A familiar feminine voice jarred him from his despondent thinking. A pair of black-and-white Vans stopped near his feet. He squinted up to find Leah smiling down at him. "You know they have chairs in the library, right?"

He summoned a lopsided smile. "Yep, I'm aware of that convenience."

"Are you aware of an even better spot to hang out? It's called the union. There's food there." She moved her head toward that building, where there was in fact food, and the better sort than the Monster he'd just drained down his throat.

"There is that as well. But I've got a class here in thirty minutes."

Not one easily deterred from her purpose, Leah reached toward him, as if to give him a hand up. "The union is a five-minute walk. That gives you twenty to sit in a nice comfy chair and catch up with me."

Brayden stared at those long fingers, tipped with bright-red nails, held out for him. Last night he'd resolved against any further interaction with Leah.

"Come on, Bray. I'm starving, and this baby isn't happy about it. You can brood over whatever it is that has you scowling while I scarf down a chicken sandwich."

"I'm not brooding."

"Even better. Brooding men are little more than pouting boys." She bent down enough to snatch his hand and then pulled. "Let's go."

Suddenly he was on his feet and then striding beside her, heading toward the union.

Leah glanced at him, smacking her gum. "You look like a mess. Was there a party last night?"

"Nope. Definitely not a party."

"Ah." She giggled the word knowingly. "Newlyweds. I know."

"Doubt it."

"Passion is passion, either way you cut it."

He squinted at her suspiciously. "You and Aiden fight much?"

"At least once a week." She winked, and then the merriment drained from her expression entirely. "Before he deployed. Now we barely speak. I get a video every now and then. A phone call here and there, one that lasts about four minutes. Can't waste that on a fight."

They reached the doors to the union, and Brayden opened it, waiting while Leah passed through before him. "I'm sorry, Leah. That must be hard."

She huffed and then shrugged. "He could have picked a different career path. One that wouldn't have him gone right now, so . . ."

There was definitely bitterness in that statement.

"Wasn't he already enlisted when you married him?"

"Yes." Leah shot him a scowl before she stepped into the Chick-fil-A line.

"Did you think that was going to change?"

"I thought he could switch career tracks. There are a lot of options in the military. But Aiden has his heart set on becoming a Ranger, and to do that, he's got to make rank in his infantry. So here we are. He's off proving he can shoot stuff up, and I'm here alone and pregnant." She glanced back at him. "Bet that puts your little fight last night in perspective, hmm?"

Maybe. Well, not much, considering his fight with Audrey had been resolved, so that was irrelevant. And Leah's little speech had clearly *not* been intended to put his marriage in perspective, but to provoke his pity for her. Had she always operated this way?

Brayden shoved his hands into his pockets, shuffling behind her as the line moved. In the space between their conversation, he pondered if he'd been blind to this bit of Leah he wasn't impressed with, or if it was a new development. He remembered a lot of fights between them. More than a few breakups. Likely, then, yeah, this was Leah. She hadn't changed. Had he been like her? Was he now?

Before he reached a conclusion, she was ordering.

". . . and two cookies and cream shakes," she finished.

He jerked his head toward her, suddenly aware of her rattling off food items. "I wasn't going to eat."

"You love their shakes. Cookies and cream is your favorite."

Brayden shook his head and then looked at the guy on the other side of the counter. "None for me."

The worker eyed him, none too pleased. "She already paid, sir."

"Yeah. I already paid, Brayden." Triumph gleamed unhindered in her blue eyes. "Just say thank you."

"I really—" *didn't want one.* Because he really didn't intend to sit with her. He shouldn't even be there with her right at that moment. If he couldn't bring himself to tell his wife, this was absolutely not a good idea. And no, he still felt like he couldn't tell Audrey about Leah being there. Especially not after their fight last night. Audrey felt too insecure with everything that had changed in her life so quickly, and frankly, he didn't feel all that stable with it himself.

Leah looped her hand through his elbow and tugged. "Stop being such a pouter and enjoy your treat." She dragged him to the end of the counter, where her food was appearing, and let him go. After she gathered her order, one lone cup of cookies and cream shake stood waiting for him to claim.

Brayden buttoned in a sigh, snagged the perspiring cup, and followed the blonde he used to date to a small round table tucked in a quiet corner.

There had been a time he'd have followed this girl blind off a cliff and never utter a word of protest. Had Leah known that?

Did she think that was still the case?

It wasn't.

With a hand on her baby bump, Leah lowered onto a seat, tossing her long hair so that it hooked behind her shoulder. Brayden set the shake he hadn't ordered onto the table but remained on his feet. As if oblivious to his silent stand against her manipulation, she emptied her paper bag, arranging her sandwich and fries without a glance at him. Right up until he backed away from the table.

"Brayden, sit." She looked up like his protest was cute but she knew his bluff. "It's five minutes of your time, which, as we both know, you weren't doing anything with anyway."

Apparently she did know his bluff. Brayden raked fingers through his hair, blew out a breath, and then jerked a chair out from the table. After sliding his backpack from his shoulders, he dropped onto the seat. "Five minutes."

"As I said." She smiled, then turned her attention to doctoring her chicken with the sauce that was her weakness. "But it can't be spent sulking, so quit slumping like the world is mean and enjoy your shake."

Brayden stabbed the frozen treat with his spoon. "Does your husband know why you transferred?" A loaded bite of chilled sugar filled his mouth. It *was* good, and maybe he was a little hungry for it.

"Of course. I told him I had a friend here, and it was closer to home. Just like I told you." Her crisp blue-eyed look jabbed up at him, brows raised. "Which is the truth, Brayden."

"You and I were never that sort of friends, Leah."

"Doesn't mean we can't be." With both hands, she lifted her sandwich and took an unladylike mouthful. Halfway through chewing it, she wiped her face with a napkin and spoke with the paper still in front of her face. "You know me better than anyone, and I'd wager I know you the same."

"Seems like all that *knowing* might make things a little complicated."

She shrugged. "Why should it?"

Was that a valid question? Did he really have a reason to think this scenario was flirting with trouble? If he did, then he needed to deal with some heart issues of his own.

Conviction zeroed in on that.

The issue with this situation was in his heart. His mind. That wasn't a good enough reason to deny Leah the only friendship she had right now, was it?

Oaf. That didn't feel right either. What would Audrey say about it? The weight of his exhaustion pressed into that thought. He wasn't up for another round of conflict with his wife. He couldn't keep going on conflict-laden evenings, sleepless nights, stupid-early mornings, and marathon-long days.

"So," Leah said before she popped a waffle fry into her mouth. "How'd you meet?"

Brayden furrowed his brow. "Huh?"

"You and your wife. What's her name?"

He leaned back against the chair. "Audrey."

"Brayden and Audrey." She tested the pairing of names, as if tasting food. Her look drifted upward, like she was deciding, and then she shrugged. "Not what I'd imagined. But whatever. How'd you meet?"

Not exactly what he'd imagined either, but they weren't gonna go into that. "She's my sister-in-law's best friend."

"She is?" Confusion crumpled her face. "Which sister-in-law?"

"Megan."

"I don't remember a Megan."

"That's because you've never met her. She married Brandon."

"Brandon got *married*?" Shock molded her expression, as if that was the last thing on the planet she would have ever guessed Brandon to do.

Brayden rolled his eyes. "Yes. Brandon is married."

"Well, you can't blame me for being surprised. He never spoke. Never dated. Frankly, he was the least fun person I've ever met. I thought he'd bach it for life."

The fierce irritation Brayden felt at Leah's assessment of his brother surprised him. After all, he'd thought nearly the same about Brandon. Leah didn't need to say things like that though. "Brandon dated some."

Truth. Brandon had gone on a few dates before he'd jumped into an arranged engagement to Megan. Though, Leah did have a point. Brandon had been a combination of introverted and hard to please that had made it easy to assume no woman on earth would neither pull him out of himself long enough to wring out a forever promise, nor would she want to put up with his stern and high expectations.

Megan had been a shocker to Brayden too. To all the Murphys. But she was good for Brandon. Even Brayden, with all his unresolved resentment toward his brother, had to admit the truth of it. Megan softened Brandon's sharp edges, and she had the singular ability to summon that brother's good humor on a consistent basis.

They were happy. Enviably happy.

God still breathed miracles. The rather deadpan thought made the corners of Brayden's mouth twitch.

"I feel like you're avoiding the question." Leah cleaned her fingers with the napkin, folded her arms, and sat back. "You have like a dozen sisters-in-law. Why this particular one's best friend?"

"I only have six brothers."

"Only." Leah snorted. "That's enough to lose count." Sitting up, she snatched her lemonade and then set a smile on Brayden that was too familiar.

Teasing. Playing. Tempting.

An old tug yanked in Brayden's chest, and before he could stop himself, he leaned in too, forearms against the table, his head swimming in that ocean-blue gaze. "Yes, only six." He spoke low. "But you never got that right. Perhaps because only one of the Murphys mattered." Did he wink? Heaven help him, what was he doing?

A flirty smirk tugged on her mouth as she chuckled softly. "You are one of a kind, Brayden Murphy. Always have been." She reached across the bit of table between them and tapped her finger on his arm. "And you may have a point."

How had this happened? They'd been talking about his family. No, they'd been talking about how he'd met his *wife*. Why was he leaning in, swimming in those blue eyes? Taking the bait like a stupid fish who only acted on the cravings of his flesh?

Hadn't he replayed this scene enough with this particular lady? More, he was *married* to Audrey. That reason alone was enough to put a stop to this rerun.

Sobering up quick, Brayden pushed backward and stood, snatching his backpack as he moved.

"Where are you going?" Leah scowled. "I still haven't heard the story."

"I met Audrey when I went to help Brandon with a job." He snatched the half-full shake. "Thanks for this. I've got class."

Leah's frown eased, and she sucked on the straw to her lemonade, her gaze light and teasing again. "Well then, off you go. Next time, you can buy."

Nope. Not gonna be a next time. Brayden's sense about this hadn't changed during that little interlude. In fact, his fish-on-a-hook reaction only confirmed what he'd already suspected. This was a bad idea.

Friends wasn't an option when it came to Leah. Whether she intended to be so or not, she was an unconverted flirt. He couldn't trust her, and, more importantly, he clearly couldn't trust himself.

He was pretty sure she knew it.

—ele—

Audrey paused near the library, squinting at the man who had just burst from the union exit, a red cup in one hand and a deep scowl evident even from the distance of a half a football field between them. As sigh pressed from her chest as her heart squeezed. What was going on with him?

With a flick of her wrist, she checked her smartwatch. Ten minutes until her next class didn't leave a whole lot of room for diversions. But Brayden was her husband. He was worth being late for. Pivoting, Audrey set her stride toward him, going double-quick to catch up.

Hunched shoulders, and a fist wrapped tight on the strap of his backpack, Brayden's get-away pace required Audrey to jog to catch up. "Hey," she called just loud enough to snag his attention.

Brayden jerked to a halt, his shoulders ramming straight. It took a moment before he turned to face her. A moment, Audrey suspected, he used to rearrange his expression into an obviously fake grin.

"Hi, babe. Aren't you heading the wrong direction?"

Shrugging, she pulled in a breath meant to cover the fact that she'd jogged to get to him. "I saw you coming from the union."

Instantly that false cheer darkened. "You . . . I—" His look moved beyond her to the building he seemed to be running from, and he frowned. "I was just grabbing a snack." Looking back at her, he held up the cup.

"I see." Audrey tipped her face to the side and studied the dark brown of his eyes. Why did his look seem shuttered? Stepping nearer, she reached to cover that clenched fist on his pack. "You okay, Bray?"

Brows drawn inward, Brayden shook his head. "Let's not do this all over again."

"I'm not looking for a fight. Just worried about you. You're upset and trying to hide it." She edged closer. "I love you, Bray. I want to be here for you."

Though his frown altered, it didn't disappear. He looked to the side and visibly swallowed. When he turned his gaze back to her, he mustered a ghost of that smile she craved. "I know. You never let me down, Audrey. Thank you." He let go of the strap he'd been clinging to and gripped her fingers. "Get to class, hon. Don't worry about me."

Audrey pulled her bottom lip between her teeth and continued to study him. Why wouldn't he tell her? She wanted so much to be in his heart, but it was like he couldn't allow it. Or wouldn't. She looked toward the tips of her shoes and then nodded. The feel of his fingers beneath her chin took her by surprise, as did the tender look she found in those brown eyes narrowed on her.

"Everything is fine. You have enough on you mind. I don't want you to worry." The pad of his thumb brushed her chin. "I'll see you at home, okay?"

She swam in that moment, his warm gaze anchored on her, his light touch a caress. Maybe she was in his heart? Perhaps it was just different than she'd expected. Or maybe he was wrestling with something and needed her to give him space to do it. That was acceptable. Everyone had things they needed to work through on their own. Or, hopefully, between God and themselves. Given the choices they'd made and the events of their lives the past several months, she and Brayden both had things they needed to deal with before God. Maybe her husband was just now coming to grips with that.

If that's so, will You help him, Father?

Heart more settled, Audrey smiled at him, took the hand that had lifted her chin, and brushed a kiss across his knuckles. "Okay. Hope the rest of your day goes well."

"You too." He squeezed her fingers and turned to go.

Audrey stood and watched his back as he moved away. He seemed less tense, and his stride wasn't a march this time. She breathed out as relief rushed in.

Brayden wasn't shutting her out. They were simply figuring out this marriage business. He was right. Everything was going to be okay.

Chapter Thirteen

(IN WHICH THE WINNER GETS ICE CREAM)

Brayden didn't like the inky sludge coursing in the pit of his gut.

Taking the longest route possible back to the apartment, he stopped at the lake on the opposite end of campus and shoved his hands into his pockets. There, he allowed the events of the past couple of days to scroll through his mind, several moments of which triggered an undeniably emotional response. Seeing Leah again. Had he craved that? Must have, by the way his chest had lurched. Not telling Audrey about it. That sour feeling was absolutely guilt, and it still festered. More so now, because when he got to the scene where Leah had him reeled in and gazing into those blue pools of temptation, that oozing muck began to burn.

Audrey deserves more.

The unavoidable fact that his wife was entitled to more than what he offered her continued to plague Brayden's mind. Disturb his heart. This shouldn't be this hard. He liked Audrey. Cared about her. Had *married* her, and they were going to have a baby. They were a family. That seemed like enough to make him forget this emotional wrestling. How much more did she expect from him? He'd already given her everything.

A painful emptiness opened in his chest, so suddenly that he placed a hand over his heart and rubbed his palm against the spot where it throbbed. He could do much more. Much better. Everything he'd offered Audrey was on the surface.

Just that afternoon, she'd seen his struggle—the one he didn't want her to know about—and had tenderly offered to help him shoulder it. *I love you, Bray.*

She was constant. Unselfish. Guileless. All opposites, as was becoming clearer with each new encounter, of Leah.

It's just the hangover of history.

That had to be it. Lingering attraction for the girl he'd once loved. *Had it been love?* Shared moments between Leah and him invaded his mind. Moments of laughter. And moments that should not have been shared between them, but still lived in a dark, back corner of his mind. Memories that he hadn't been able to banish entirely yet. Brayden moved his palm from his chest, slid it up his neck, and then rubbed the side of his jaw. A year ago, that question about loving Leah would have had an unreserved answer. Today, not so much. Either way, it didn't matter.

Audrey mattered. He focused on the memories he and Audrey shared. There weren't enough of them to outweigh what had accumulated between Leah and himself. That, he could fix. And he would.

With a fresh sense of purpose, and determination for it refueled, Brayden gave the lake and its fountain his back and strode back the way he'd come. The long route home was no longer needed as the inky sludge of guilt settled into a place that was ignorable. Brayden lengthened his stride, now eager to get home to his wife.

After slipping into the apartment and dumping his backpack on a chair in the dining room, he went in search of the girl who had taken his last name. He found Audrey in their bedroom, a mound of unfolded laundry heaped in the middle of their bed. Stopping at her back, he hooked his arms around her shoulders and pulled her against himself.

"Hi." Her greeting held a smile. One that hinted toward relief, like she'd expected him to come home in a testy mood.

Brayden bent his neck and grazed his lips against the soft skin near her ear. Inhaling, he shut his eyes and committed her sweet scent to memory. What was it?

"You smell good," he murmured.

Audrey lowered the shirt she'd lifted before her to snap straight before folding and melted backward into him. "I do?"

"Yes." He nuzzled his nose deeper into her neck and inhaled again. "What is it?"

"Sweet Peas. A gift from Megan—they're her favorite. She gets the bubble bath, the body wash, the lotion, the body spray."

"Which one am I enjoying on you?"

"The body wash. It's all I have."

"Hmm." He tightened his hold on her. "Perhaps your husband should remedy that."

Though she gripped his forearms near his elbows, he felt her retreat in the space of silence she let hang.

"Or maybe that's Megan's favorite scent, but not yours?" He loosened his hold and stepped back. Then he turned her by her shoulders to face him.

Audrey shrugged. "I don't know that I have a favorite." Her gaze up at him turned long and studious.

It took intention for Brayden not to pull away, to break eye contact, or to think of something distracting to move them past this moment where it seemed his wife took inventory of his heart. Why would it be so unsettling to stand there unshielded before her? He didn't have a sure the answer to that, but at length it became too unnerving.

"Are you assessing my soul?" He hitched a crooked grin.

Laying both palms against his chest, Audrey's intense look softened into a gentle smile. "Perhaps. And you let me."

He swallowed. What clever, distracting retort could he slap on that?

Audrey must have sensed his building wave of panic. Lifting to her toes, she pressed a light kiss against his lips and then stepped back. "I'm glad your day ironed out." Then she palmed the edge of his jaw, ran a thumb along his mouth, and smiled in full.

When she turned back to the laundry, Brayden breathed a controlled breath of relief. Relief? From what? What was this fear that had gripped him under Audrey's examination? Scratching the back of his head, Brayden chased away the disruptive questions. Not what he was after. He stepped beside Audrey, reached for a shirt, and freed it from the pile.

"This is quite a mound we've accumulated."

"Yeah. Sorry about that. You must wonder what kind of lazy-dazey you married."

"What?" He looked across his shoulder at her.

"I let almost two weeks go by." Audrey shook her head, as if scolding herself. "It's amazing we aren't both running around naked."

Brayden shot his brows up, and he grinned. "That seems like a good goal to aim for next time."

"No." Her look at him was stern. "I am not that pathetic."

"Who said laundry is your responsibility, anyway?"

Now her expression was all surprise, making him chuckle.

"I know how to wash *and* fold clothes, my old-fashioned little wife. My mother wasn't about to be a slave to laundry for seven boys and a husband. She assigned each of us a day, and we had to wash our own stuff."

Surprised turned up to full-blown shock. "Your mom?"

"Yep, my mom. The one you apparently think of as June Cleaver. She made her boys do housework. Said we were not going to grow up unable to wash our own underwear."

"Hmm." Audrey's hum carried relief. "I don't really know your family, I guess."

Oh boy. There was a hint in that. One he wasn't going to indulge that evening. They were making memories, was the plan, and not ones of an argument. *Does getting to know your family have to be an argument?*

Be gone, intrusive thoughts.

"Know what else I grew up doing?" Setting aside the third shirt he folded, Brayden reached for a pair of socks, the match revealed when Audrey had snatched up a pair of her jeans to fold.

"Can it please be making a three-course meal?"

"No, sorry to disappoint you. I can grill though. Baking is out, however. That one is on you."

Her glance contained a merry grin. "Okay then. What was it you were going to say?"

"Battleship."

"Battleship?"

"Yep. Battleship. Brandon and I played almost every day."

"Are you hinting at something."

"No." He hip-checked her. "I'm telling you I want to play Battleship."

"With me?"

"Not interested?"

"No, just . . . surprised?"

"It'll be fun. Especially when we put a wager on it."

"Did you always bet on Battleship?"

"Yep. Winner gets to slug the loser."

"Your mother was good with that?"

"She didn't raise sissies, lady."

"No," Audrey said dryly. "Just men who could do laundry."

"And fell trees. And build stuff. And shoot things. And grill. And take a brotherly punch. Sometimes an angry-brother smackdown."

"All admirable. But I'm not playing for punching privileges, mister."

"Good, because I don't want to tell people my wife beat me up." He winked. "I have something else in mind." Smirking, Brayden lifted a suggestive brow.

Heat washed her face in a pretty, almost irresistible shade of pink, which she tried to hide by feigning profound interest in the remaining clothes to be folded. Brayden was not having that. He caught her chin with the tips of his fingers and positioned her face so that he could examine it.

"You're blushing, wife." He leaned in close and lowered his voice to a whisper. "What could you possibly be thinking to wager that would make you blush?"

"You're teasing me, trying to make me blush."

Brayden edged nearer. "That is true. I'm apparently good at it."

Audrey took her bottom lip with her teeth, and her eyes moved to his mouth. As his gut tightened, pleasant heat pumped through Brayden's veins. But chemistry hadn't been the issue with them. Obviously.

She deserved more from him. This marriage *needed* more.

Keeping that in mind, he dipped to indulge in a lingering kiss. He savored the sweetness of her response. Tender and yielding. Tempting him, as ever, to take more. But this evening wasn't about him taking.

Gripping self-control as he rarely had, Brayden eased away. "I don't think we were imagining the same wager, though I am quite curious about what you had in mind."

A mildly irritated smirk shaped her mouth as she shook her head and turned back to finish folding the clothes.

"Not gonna share?"

Beneath rosy cheeks, she pinned her lips closed.

Brayden sighed dramatically. "Sad. Here's my idea though. Ice cream."

"Ice cream?"

"Winner gets ice cream."

At that she turned a mild pout up to him. "What does the loser get?"

Stepping to put away his clothes, he shrugged. "To feed the winner their ice cream."

"That sounds . . . precarious."

"Perhaps." He turned back to her and winked. "Shall we find out?"

"I like ice cream."

"Then you'll have to beat me."

With a stubborn set of her chin, Audrey returned his gaze. "It's on."

———*ele*———

He clearly hadn't expected to lose.

Audrey chuckled to herself as she watched Brayden dip three obnoxiously large scoops of ice cream into a mixing bowl. "It looks like you think I'll share with you or something." She leaned her chin on his bicep and looked up at him.

"I can't believe you sank all my boats and I only nailed two of yours. That reeks of fraud."

"Did you just call me a cheater?" She snatched the bowl away and gave him her back.

Both arms circled her waist from behind, and he drew her up against him. Audrey could barely school a giggle.

"Let's just say that you can smother all suspicions with an act of diplomacy."

She squirmed free of his hold and loaded her spoon with a heaping helping of chunky monkey. "Diplomacy? That was war. It's in the name—*Battleship*. You lost."

Hands on her hips, he backed her until she bumped against the counter. "I did. Loser feeds the winner. Hand it over."

"Not on your life, buddy."

"Wife," he growled, even as his eyes danced with laughter.

"Oh." Audrey raised her loaded spoon. "Did you want some of this?"

"Nice wives share with their husbands."

"Hmm." She slipped the spoon into her mouth and then shut her eyes, making a show of her moaning pleasure. "So good," she said around her full mouth.

Brayden snatched the spoon.

"Hey!"

His chuckle was nothing short of wicked as he reloaded the spoon. "Someone needs practice sharing."

After setting aside the bowl, Audrey reached for the spoon.

"Oh, did you want this?" he mocked, pulling it out of her reach.

She took the bait. When she moved in closer to stretch for the spoon, Brayden wrapped her in a hold of containment. The mischief in his expression was all little boy. "Here. This is how we share, wife." Then he dotted her nose with a cold clump of cream.

"Brayden!"

"More?" Next, her chin.

Audrey squealed and wiggled, causing the spoon to smear against her cheek. A full belly laugh erupted from her gut, though she continued to fight against him. "Bray! Stop! You're making a mess of me!"

The spoon clattered into the bowl near her hip as Brayden's chuckle deepened. "Know what else my mother taught me?"

"I can't imagine," Audrey said breathlessly.

"To clean up my messes." Suddenly, as his brown gaze narrowed on her, the little boy vanished. His mouth found the cream on her cheek, her nose, then her chin, lingering on each spot. Audrey softened against him, and his hands claimed her in a much different hold than containment. When his lips closed on hers, the ice cream was forgotten.

And remained so for the rest of the night.

Chapter Fourteen

(IN WHICH SOMETIMES WE REGRET OUR CHOICES)

September eased forward, bringing slightly cooler temperatures to the day and definitely cooler nights. Fall colors peeked through the glossy greens of a wearied summer landscape, the oranges and reds of maples and the yellows of cottonwoods, oaks, and honey locusts a happy welcome to the changing seasons.

Once a week since the beginning of the month, Audrey indulged in the seasonal caramel pecan lattes, decaf, of course, offered at the union. It was a relief to be able to enjoy the treats without an unsettled stomach for it—that particular issue *finally* easing off, though well after she thought it should. Now she could hardly keep her stomach satisfied. Seemed the baby stole all her calories. The little imp.

As she dropped down the steps from the student center, making her way back to the medical side of campus, Audrey covered the growing little one in her womb with a hand and felt a soft kick. This little imp, as she'd taken to calling him or her, had become significantly more active. At least, she was more aware of it. She suspected boy or girl, this baby would be all Murphy, busy doing things, exploring, teasing, and generally taking after its daddy.

Her thoughts turned to that man, and she glanced around, searching faces as she walked the pathway, wondering if she'd bump into him. Brayden had seemed more settled in the past weeks, though he was still more reserved than she'd known him to be before. Then again, she'd basically known him at a distance, spending in-person time with him on weekends when he came to visit her under the guise of working with his brother. And back then . . . Well, their relationship had been more fire than foundational, even before they'd taken things too far. Perhaps living with a person day in and day out could reveal a different side of them.

She was passing between the stadium and the tennis courts when Brayden's profile drew her attention. Goodness but the man she married was handsome. Medium tall with the lean bulk of a guy who could do manual labor when life required it. Dark hair the color of an untainted bold brew and trimmed beard catching the light of the afternoon sun, showing hints of burnt orange hidden within the rich dark brown. Perhaps their son or daughter would be a redhead. Not the strawberry blond of her hair, but a rich, dark auburn. The perfect blend of her and Bray. Pausing her onward trek to class, Audrey admired the view, waiting for him to glance her direction and smile.

Smile he did. Full—the way she'd hoped. But not at her. Whoever had caught his attention and summoned his grin remained hidden behind the curve of the stadium. Brayden adjusted his course so that he walked that direction, rather than toward Audrey. Disappointment was a twist in her chest. Audrey lifted her hot latte, inhaled the bittersweet aroma of sugared coffee, and took a sip.

Oh well. She'd see him later that night at their apartment two blocks from campus. Perhaps he'd have time and energy between studying for a sunset walk around the lake. Maybe even an evening stop at the union on their way back home to grab a treat of ice cream. Then, home. He'd study, and so would she, and then they'd go to bed, not much past nine. Ten, if he could last that long. Usually, he couldn't. Four a.m. came awful early.

Tomorrow, they'd do the same all over again. Work. Classes. Home. Study.

Audrey hoped tomorrow he'd glance at her as their paths neared, and he'd smile. As she did so, she wondered who had been receiving such a happy look from her husband that day. That twist in her chest moved again, pinching harder. This time, not simply disappointment. Audrey didn't pin a label on the sharp pain though. Instead, she walked toward her principles of nutrition class.

"Did you get one for me?"

A cheerful voice filled the void and stole Audrey's thoughts from the precipice of a slippery slope. Though she glanced to her right, a look wasn't required to know to whom it belonged. She smiled at the shorter dark-haired woman who had snuck into step beside Audrey.

"I didn't, Victoria. I'm sorry." Audrey nudged her shoulder with her elbow. "Next time I'll text you to ask."

Victoria's glossy black hair gleamed as her ponytail swished in the sunlight. "You look better this week than you did when we first met. Is the baby behaving itself now?"

Audrey laughed. It was so good to have a friend who asked about her baby. So good to be able to talk about the baby with joy and anticipation.

Surely Brayden was about ready to tell their families by now. How much longer could they wait? She brushed the annoyance aside.

"This baby is hungry all the time. At this point, I can't eat enough."

"Making up for lost time, when you didn't feel like eating." Together, they turned toward the college of nursing building, which housed the human development class that was next on her schedule.

Victoria was in her twelfth month of the accelerated sixteen-month program and was at least three years older than Audrey. The age gap didn't seem to divide them—a normal situation for Audrey. Most—no, all—of the people closest to her were at least two years her senior. Usually more.

"Did you get that ultrasound scheduled yet?"

"No." Audrey's response dipped down, along with her mood. She was well past the point when they should have had imaging. Even if she hadn't already known that to be the case, her doctor had pushed for it. She'd delayed her orders though, wanting Brayden to be there for it. "My husband is so busy. We can't seem to come up with a time when he's not at work or at class." True story, there.

"Certainly he could take an hour off to go see your baby's first pictures."

"One would think." Audrey bit back the rest. It'd been a bumpy topic, and she couldn't understand why exactly. Well, maybe she could. Brayden was working himself to exhaustion trying to make sure she and their little one would be taken care of, especially since his student insurance didn't allow for a maternity rider after the fact. The only possible way they'd have this delivery covered by insurance was if she remained on her parents' plan. Since they hadn't told her parents about the baby, that was obviously not an option.

They'd have to pay for this. Or seek Medicaid. Brayden had put a hard *no* on that. Audrey didn't see how they were reasonably going to avoid it, but she didn't fight him. Time would tell, she figured.

Audrey sighed. "Ah well." Reaching for the door to the building, she brightened. "Everything seems to be okay. The little imp is busy enough, and I feel human again. An ultrasound would be fun, but right now I'm not sure it's necessary."

Victoria frowned, eyeing her. "I think I should meet this husband of yours."

Laughing off her friend's implied threat, Audrey strode toward the stairs. "Someday you should do that. If I can ever catch him standing still for more than thirty seconds."

"Oh, it's gonna happen, my friend." Vitoria lifted a sassy grin. "And he'll find out real fast that I am not nearly as agreeable as you are."

Audrey wondered how that situation would play out. Brayden wasn't a moody person—he usually gave as good as he got. But he also wasn't the type to be strong-armed. She recalled interactions between Brayden and Megan—and then Brayden and Brandon. Yikes.

It likely would not go well at all.

ele

Misgivings had given way to comfortable familiarity shortly after Labor Day. Two weeks past that point, and Brayden still wasn't entirely sure how Leah had managed that—other than to say the woman was extraordinarily persistent. She had managed to locate him on a daily basis, though he'd purposefully altered routes and study locations, and she had bribed him with treats he wouldn't have bought for himself. Mostly his favorite shakes. And beef jerky.

She knew way too much about him.

Leah knew how to work this deal. Even with that knowledge, Brayden found himself easy in her company, sliding back into old familiarity. Like a holey pair of sweats that should have been tossed ages ago, but simplicity and comfort won out.

When Leah waved at him from across the walk to the union, he'd smiled. A genuine, happy-to-see her smile that felt good. Brayden had grown tired of scowling, was weary of battling anxiety—and that over more than one thing. Audrey wanted to tell their families about the baby, and he understood why. For her, it was moving forward, embracing the life ahead of them. But he hadn't overcome the shadowed part of it.

His family would be suspicious of him, of their marriage. Simply put, he didn't want to feel it from them. He didn't want to feel their disappointment and their scorn. He didn't want to feel like the fallen brother, the one who'd messed up most. And that didn't even take into account her family. Tim had only once had a conversation with him since the day Brayden had moved Audrey out. It had been strained at best, a halting, fatherly commission to take care of his daughter, and please make sure she finishes school.

Brayden could only imagine how it would go when they told her father she was pregnant. A mother at nineteen, thanks to Brayden's willful irresponsibility and rebellion. Even now, the thought made his gut split.

All this put stress into the relationship he shared with his wife. Not necessarily her fault, and he knew it, but the few hours he spent with Audrey were often passed with an underlying tension.

Tension that did not exist with Leah.

There was danger there, and Brayden knew it. But there was also relief. Couldn't he have a friend with whom there was no undercurrent of stress? As long as he kept things simple—kept forefront what this friendship was and what it wasn't, it'd be fine.

Everything was fine.

"How about coffee?" Leah met him at the midpoint of the stadium, her arm slipping into the crook of his as she spun to face the direction he was moving. Falling into step beside him, they made their way together toward the union.

"Coffee?" He glanced down at her with a skeptical look, his gaze intentionally moving to the swell of her belly and then back to her face. "Is that a good idea?"

Leah shrugged. "I'll go half-caf."

"You're studying to be a PA. Surely you already know caffeine isn't ideal for the baby."

"Millions of women drink full strength every day of their pregnancy and have healthy babies. Let's not go overboard. Anyway, the studies are inconclusive."

"Hmm." Audrey had gone cold turkey off caffeine, largely at his urging. He'd read an article in a medical journal about miscarriage, preterm birth, and low birthweight associated with caffeine. Granted, the article stated that the association wasn't conclusive, but it urged caution where there was uncertainty. Not usually Brayden's route of choice in life, but this was Audrey and their baby under consideration. So caution it was.

However, Leah wasn't *his* wife, and her choices were her own. Brayden shrugged away an urge to persuade her from her more caviler attitude about it. Not his rodeo, as his mom would say. Instead, he switched topics. "When are you due, anyway?"

"December." Leah looked off into the distance, unsmiling.

"Is there a problem with December?"

"Aiden won't be back by then."

"Oh." He bumped her shoulder with his. "I'm sorry. That's gotta be hard for both of you. I'm sure it bothers him as much as it bothers you."

"Yeah. Well, like I said before, he could have made other choices."

"The universal disclaimer." Brayden pressed his lips closed after that slipped out.

Leah tipped her face to settle those blue eyes on him. The regret in her gaze reached in and gripped the inside of his chest, instantly making him wish he'd not said those words. Setting his jaw, he kept his eyes firmly forward, even when she leaned into his arm, laying her head against his shoulder. As his bicep flexed, Brayden eased away until Leah dropped her touch entirely.

He hadn't intended to imply anything. Clearly Leah thought otherwise.

For several strides, silence stretched between them. Moments during which Brayden reconsidered what exactly he was doing, indulging in this friendship. Leah didn't know boundaries. Frankly, Brayden hadn't been very good at them either. This wasn't a game they could play anymore though. He had so much more to lose than he'd ever had before. And, to be clear, he didn't want to lose.

Audrey mattered to him. Deeply, greatly. More so as the days passed. Her quiet, persistent love was unselfish and admittedly undeserved. Brayden had been his worst self with her on more than one occasion. Rather than sulking or holding his failures against him, Audrey forgave and continued to love. She made Brayden want better. For himself, *of* himself, for her and for their baby. He wanted to be the Murphy Audrey had believed him to be.

Wanting that and *being* that, though . . . Why exactly did he struggle so hard? Seemed like his brothers were intuitively good, and equally blessed for it. What Brayden saw of their stories made life out like everything should just be easy. Easy choices. Easy paths. The Murphy legacy. Except not with him. It was like all the goodness ran out after Brandon was born, that brother having a particularly strong dose of Murphy morality, and Brayden hadn't been endowed with a whole lot to work with.

"I'm glad you brought up the due date." Hesitancy laced Leah's voice as she broke the awkward silence between them. "I have a favor to ask."

Not a good lead. Brayden steeled himself.

"Like I said, Aiden's not going to be back by then. And as I've told you, you're my only friend around here . . ."

Brayden stopped just before they reached the steps leading to the student center. Facing Leah, he shook his head. "No."

"No?" She smiled that trademark, take-his-breath-away smile. The one that usually guaranteed she'd get her way. "I haven't even asked anything yet."

He held a long, challenging stare on her, knowing exactly what she was going to ask. Leah studied him back, charming smile fading, her expression molding toward confusion by his immediate response to a question he deemed wildly inappropriate. After several breaths where her gaze turned from manufactured perplexity to silent pleading, she edged backward, letting her now disappointed look drift toward his shoes.

"You can't do this, Leah." Brayden hooked a thumb onto the strap of his backpack.

"Do what?"

"You know exactly what I'm talking about. You can't manipulate me and expect that we're going to be friends. And you can't ask things of me that you know well and good would upset the people in our lives that we care about."

"It was just a backup plan. For if I go into labor and my mom can't make it in time."

"I'm not your backup plan." Not anymore. Not ever again.

Leah lifted her chin, pain passing over her expression, as if she understood the many layers of that statement.

Choices. They had both made choices. Maybe she regretted hers. But Brayden . . .

Yeah, he had regrets. But right then he understood more clearly than ever that losing Leah was no longer top on that list. Maybe it didn't make the cut at all anymore. Though there was tension in his marriage, Audrey didn't do this—she didn't play games, didn't manipulate him. Didn't reel him in just to toss him back.

Brayden pivoted as if to head back to the med center. He could grab a coffee from the machine on the first floor of the health sciences building. With a glance at his wrist, he checked the time. He might even catch Audrey before she slipped into her nutrition class.

As he stepped away, Leah grabbed his arm. "Coffee, remember?"

"I'm gonna go."

"Come on, Bray. Let's forget this little . . . tiff. It's fine. I'll find someone else to call. No worries, okay?"

Was she speaking as if she *forgave* him for not agreeing to her ludicrous request?

She must have sensed his building irritation with her. "Look, I'm sorry." Her hold on his arm switched to patting his shoulder. "Just blame it on hormones. Me not thinking straight. Okay?"

He should be striding away. Heading toward his wife. Instead, he remained planted, turning back to look at Leah. Relenting.

"I'll buy you that coffee, and we'll forget about this." Blue eyes and that trademark smile. Always the hook.

She just needs a friend.

Brayden couldn't decern if that was a stupid excuse or a divine nudge. Either way, he sighed and then followed her into the union.

Later, as he walked the long route home, hoping to smother the roiled sludge that had flared in his gut, he focused on Audrey. On his marriage. And on how to keep his heart and mind on the path he knew was right.

It'd been a few weeks since he and Audrey had laughed. Since he'd teased and flirted with her. It was time for another round of Battleship, he thought. Battleship, and ice cream, and whatever followed after that.

Chapter Fifteen

(IN WHICH THE HEARTBREAK IS TOO MUCH)

Audrey arched her back as she leaned away from the table where her laptop sat. She'd been studying for over an hour, hunched over the screen, reading text until it blurred before her. The ache in her back told her it was time to stretch. As she spun on the chair to rise, her hand spread over the swell of the baby.

The little imp has been awfully still today.

The thought was jarring. When was the last time she'd felt the baby move?

A chill draped her as panic clutched her heart. Audrey went through her day, moment by moment, from the time she'd risen from bed. As was usual, Brayden had already been gone, the spot where he'd slept beside her cold. She'd texted him good morning, then made a honeyed white tea to go with toast and eggs for breakfast. Her Bible had been open beside her plate as she ate her breakfast and read Isaiah 54.

Pausing there, Audrey had shut her eyes and summoned the verse that had called to her heart that morning. "'Though the mountains be shaken and the hills be removed, yet my unfailing love for you will not be shaken nor my covenant of peace be removed,' says the Lord, who has compassion on you."

As the verse passed through her mind, Audrey's hands trembled. Why had that particular verse been in her morning reading? In the middle of a passage calling out encouragement to people in the midst of despair, why had it called to her heart?

The stillness within her womb seemed to whisper an answer.

"Oh God," Audrey whimpered.

A rustling sounded from the couch, followed by a glimpse of Brayden's pillow-mussed hair as he sat up. "Audrey? You okay?"

"The baby hasn't moved."

"What?"

"I don't think the baby has moved all day." She continued to scan her activities. Walking to the medical center, going to class. Lunch with Victoria.

"All day? Not at all?"

Tears flooded her eyes, and her mind raced to recall the rest of the day. No bouncing, rhythmic hiccups. No rolling. No sporadic jabs. Nothing stood out. Not a squirm leapt into those memories. "I don't remember," she replied breathlessly. A sudden sob cracked through her chest, and she folded forward, wrapping her arms around her middle. How had she not noticed until now?

Several footfalls sounded against the floor, and then Brayden was there, hands on her shoulders, kneeling in front of her, face searching hers. "Don't panic, hon. Maybe it's nothing. Maybe there was something you just don't remember."

"Brayden, something's wrong. I feel it in my heart." As desperation filled her being, she searched the brown eyes that held her in his steady, concerned gaze.

His palms slid on either side of her jaw, thumbs brushing over her cheeks. "Shh. Don't cry now. We'll go right now and see, okay?"

By then Audrey was crying in earnest, warm tears a steady flow that wet her cheeks, covering his thumbs. He pulled her head into his shoulder and then wrapped her in a tight hold against him. "God, we need You. We're begging for mercy here, Lord. Please let everything be okay."

Her racing heart slowed as Brayden's hoarse words touched her ears. He'd never done that. Never prayed with her, other than the standard *thanks for the day and this food* over their occasionally shared meals. Not once. Truthfully, Audrey had come to wonder if their faith was really a shared thing between them. Or rather, feared that Brayden's was little more than a borrowed idea he'd gotten from his family. Standard Murphy issue.

But here, in their moment crisis, he'd turned straight to God. That was something, wasn't it? A thing to lift in broken praise, even while she silently begged God for exactly what Brayden had asked.

Mercy, Father. Please. I know we didn't do things like we should have. But I love this baby. We love this child. Please . . .

Brayden stood, pulling her to her feet as he moved. Then with a protective arm around her shoulders, he guided her out of their apartment and down to the parked car. Frightened silence filled the vehicle as Brayden drove to the hospital. Dread, thick and chilled, pressed into Audrey's heart.

That passage she'd read that morning, it'd been filled with the contradiction of heartache and God's promise of unwavering love. As she'd read it, she'd gripped the unwavering love part. Smiled into it. How easy it had been to skim over the heartache part.

She didn't want the heartache part.

Please, not the heartache part.

As Brayden parked and then jogged around the front of the car to her side, the sense of foreboding flooded her heart until it seemed that was all she knew. This was not going to end as she wanted, as she'd pleaded.

How was she going to handle the heartbreak her gut warned her was coming?

—ele—

Helplessness was a violent unmooring. A tempest that, in the space of a few moments, had taken Brayden from a relatively steady confidence that though he wasn't the man his brothers were, eventually life would work out, to a shattering reality that some things just didn't. With Audrey's hand wrapped securely in his, tucked firmly against his chest, he peeked at the screen that the tech had turned away from Audrey's view and knew for certain his desperate grasping at hope had been vanity. This, the first image of their baby, was devastatingly still. A child in miniature, curled in his wife's womb, fists tucked against his head—and no heartbeat to be found.

His son had died, and he'd never gotten to hold him. Never had even glimpsed the miraculous form when he'd kicked and squirmed and grew.

The heart within him ripped apart, and he could not stop the quivering of his jaw. Brayden moved his eyes from the screen to Audrey, who had been watching him. Tears were rivers on her face, brokenness a new and awful dullness in her eyes. His heart rent again, the searing pain stealing his breath.

Why, God?

The silent cry barely filled his mind before being drowned by a dark guilt. All the things he'd done wrong. His stubborn, rebellious path led him here. Worse, he'd taken Audrey straight into this agony with him.

Would God do this? Take his son and shatter his wife's heart, in retribution?

Brayden squeezed his burning eyes shut as these thoughts, these accusations, these questions became emotions too dark and heavy to navigate. He couldn't think to find answers. There was only feeling. Awful, suffocating feeling, and he crumpled beneath the weight.

A whisper of Audrey's sob reached through the blackness wrapping around Brayden. Raising his eyes to her, he reached to cup her soaked face. Only broken silence existed in the heartache they'd not expected.

The tech finished, shut down her equipment, and moved toward the door. "You can get dressed and go back to the waiting room. The doctor will call you back to speak with you soon."

Get dressed and go sit in the waiting room? Couldn't they stay there, hidden from the rest of the world while they waited for the news they'd never wanted to hear? The door clicked closed, and he and Audrey were alone.

"Bray." Her airy voice begged for comfort. "Did you see a heartbeat?"

The knife cut fresh, his heart becoming confetti with each slice. He didn't want to tell her. Who wanted to speak such awful things?

And he thought he wanted to be a doctor? Suddenly the prospect held little appeal. The routine wasn't simply science put into practice. It was diving into this terrible place where people's most dreadful moments existed. It was shouldering their hardest burdens and, worse, being the one to tell them the worst news of their lives.

He couldn't do it. Not with his own wife, not about their unborn son. The words wouldn't even form in his mind, let alone escape past the swelling of his throat. Instead, Brayden leaned in, gathered her close, and held her while a fresh round of sobs shook through her body.

Why would You do this?

Again, that inky feeling of guilt smothered his heavenward inquiry. This was his fault. Audrey, sobbing in his arms, was his fault. He had brought them to this moment, and up until this moment had been mostly unrepentant for it.

How could a man bear up under such a thing?

Audrey clung to him, grasping for comfort, though there surely was none to be had. Not from him, at least. He had done nothing but lead her into ruin. Had taken this vibrant, sweet young woman and twisted her promising future into this broken heart.

At some point, she'd realize that.

How could a man live with that?

Brayden couldn't find answers to his desperate questions any more than he could make this horrible thing go away.

So they did the next thing. Audrey traded the hospital gown for her clothing. He guided her back to the waiting room, where he fought to hold the fragmented pieces of himself together while they sat with three strangers on the worst night of his life. Then they were called back to another room.

The walk to the patient room felt like passing from one life to another. Going from mostly carefree bliss to a sadness that would scar them for life. There, in that cold room, a man, a stranger, spoke in a voice that portrayed a strange concoction of compassion and detachment, his announcement like the clanking of a steel door behind them. The final step of this quick and unwanted journey.

The doctor left, telling them to take their time. When they were ready, a nurse would guide them to LDR, and the next phase of this nightmare would commence.

How would they ever be ready?

Brayden steeled himself. Sought for that detached place he'd detected in the doctor who had delivered the news. He didn't know how else to get through this. Especially as the hours wore on and he witnessed Audrey go from emotionally devastated into intense physical pain as she labored to bring forth their son.

He could scarcely bear it, witnessing her pain and struggle. It would have been one thing to do so with the promise of new life on the other side. But there wasn't.

There was only the heartache of holding a tiny, perfectly formed baby boy, whom he would never watch grow into a man. Only the shattering reality of losing his son. And seeing his wife devastated.

How could there be life and joy after that?

Chapter Sixteen

(IN WHICH THE TRUTH BECOMES KNOWN)

Devastation swept Audrey into a sea of emptiness in the days following. The physical recovery from delivery and the painful swelling of her breasts were constant, unavoidable reminders. Even sleep, which was where she retreated often, was a place of deep ache. Images of her baby boy, all of one pound, eight ounces and fitting easily in the hollow of Brayden's cupped hands, met her in place of dreams. A baby's cries, distinctly newborn, would wake her.

How was she to survive this loss?

Alone, it seemed.

While Brayden had wept with her in the hospital and had been tender in the days after she'd been discharged, he was also significantly more detached. He took no time off work or school, had few words to share over supper, and studied longer while shut up in a separate room until he finally crawled into bed next to her at a much later hour than his norm. The time before, when Audrey had felt he'd cut her off, was nothing compared to this.

She needed someone.

The third day home from the hospital, Megan called. It took less than five seconds for her best friend to know Audrey wasn't okay.

"What's going on?" Megan asked.

Audrey collapsed into a sob. "Oh, Meg . . ."

"Audrey." Panic was a dart in her voice. "Talk to me."

Drawing a shuddering breath, Audrey fought to push words past her tight, swollen throat. "I was pregnant."

Patient silence waited on the other end of the call.

"Was. Megan . . . my son . . . my son died."

"Oh, Audrey." Tears cracked in Megan's voice. "Oh, my sweet friend. I'm so sorry. We didn't know."

No one knew. Because Brayden had refused to tell the truth. No one knew, and now Audrey was all alone, lost in a sea of grief.

"Hang on, sweetie. I'm calling Brandon as soon as we hang up, and then we're coming."

Audrey sniffed. "I'm not sure Bray—"

"He doesn't get a say this time. I'm coming, Audrey. Be there in a couple of hours. Or less."

This time Audrey didn't argue. She couldn't say anything at all.

"I love you, my friend. Be there soon, okay?"

Nodding with the phone against her cheek, Audrey whispered, "Thanks." Then the call ended.

As Audrey curled onto her bed, tucking a fat pillow beneath her head and clinging to it with both arms, relief at Megan's bold insistence mixed with a hint of dread. Audrey had no idea how Brayden would handle his brother and Megan showing up in the middle of their crisis. By all other interactions between Brayden and Brandon, she suspected her husband wasn't going to welcome the visitors.

But as Megan said, this time Brayden didn't get a choice. In the most heartbreaking way possible, the truth had become known. He could do nothing about that, just as she could do nothing to bring back her son.

Audrey shut her eyes and willed blank sleep to claim her until Megan and Brandon showed up. She didn't want to worry about Brayden and his issues with his brother. Not any more than she wanted this piercing pain to continue in her heart.

_ℓℓ_

Keep going. Just do the next thing. This was all Brayden knew to do. Though exhaustion poisoned his body and rode hard on his already jagged emotions, he continued. Work. School. Home. Study. Sleep—but not much of that.

In all of that, there was worry on top of heartbreak. Audrey had understandably slipped into the grips of grief in a way that had changed her from a generally happy, positive person to one who didn't leave the apartment. As yet, she barely made it out of bed. He'd found he had to wake her up, and he did so hesitantly, to feed her something at suppertime. That he did only because he worried she wasn't eating at all when he wasn't there to ensure she had something nourishing her recovering body.

He envied her retreat into sleep but didn't begrudge it. Though, he wondered how much rest she truly got. When he checked on her after classes, before he started making supper, he had found traces of dried tears near her nose and at the corners of her eyes. At night, she would cry softly in her sleep.

Grief was a hard thing. There was no shortcut through it and no way to know exactly how long the darkest hour of it would last. Brayden had consulted the pamphlets the nurse had supplied them on discharge. *Navigating loss. Miscarriage and recovery.* Both well intentioned, certainly. And perhaps helpful, though he was still thrashing too hard at the shock to know for certain. Could one truly navigate this sort of thing? That implied control over the journey. He had none. Nor did Audrey. They were subject to the winds and tides of this storm.

The pamphlets advised working to remain close. To share the burden of loss together.

Brayden wanted to. Were it not for the mountain of guilt that had surged upward within, perhaps he could. As it was, he could do little more than reach across the space of mattress between him and his wife to stroke her hair while she whimpered in her sleep. He could make sure she had at least a little bit to eat every day. And he could make sure he had money to pay the bills that would keep her housed, fed, and in school while he worked toward a better future.

Those things he could do. But he couldn't lay before her his broken heart. Not when he knew hers was every bit as shattered, and this whole thing was his fault. If not for him, she'd be a blissful freshman student at a school of her choosing. She'd be looking forward to fall break, a time she'd share with the parents she had a good relationship with, and between whom he'd driven a wedge.

If not for him, Audrey wouldn't know any of this brokenness.

Such thoughts plagued him. Paralyzed him.

Lost in them once again, Brayden stared out of the windshield of his parked car. Another day had scraped by. Up those stairs to his left, he'd enter the home he shared with the girl he'd ruined, hope that this time she'd be awake and not quite so drawn and pale, and likely as not, find her instead curled in a fetal position on their bed.

The now-familiar piercing arrow stung his heart, and he shut his eyes.

Navigate this? Not likely.

With a ragged sigh, he unclenched the grip he held on the steering wheel, wearily reached for the backpack occupying the passenger seat, then let himself out of the car. Feet like cast-iron weights, he trudged up the steps and jammed his key into the door to his apartment.

It wasn't locked.

For the first time in days, a crack of lighted hope broke through his darkness. Audrey was up then. Swallowing against the swell of emotion that unexpected possibility provoked, Brayden turned the knob and slipped into his home. He kicked off his shoes, lowered the pack to the floor, and then went looking for his wife. As he'd dared to hope, she was up, sitting on the couch.

As he'd *not* at all expected, she was not alone.

A jolt that seemed an awful lot like one would feel after suddenly stepping into a snare rammed through his chest. Brayden stopped short.

"Megan."

A rustling sounded from the chair that sat opposite where he stood, and then Brandon appeared, lifting from that seat and pivoting to face Brayden.

"Hi, Brayden." Megan spoke softly, not moving from her place on the sofa next to Audrey. Her hand held Audrey's, and her blue eyes settled on him with nothing short of pity.

Brayden wasn't sure what he felt, though there was emotion aplenty crashing over him. Clenching his jaw, he moved his look to Audrey. His wife merely glanced at him before her focus drifted back to her hands. "Megan called earlier. I needed to tell someone."

Chest collapsing, Brayden refused to process that statement. If he did, there would surely be more guilt. He couldn't scale what was already before him as it was. He moved his gaze to Brandon, who stood as guardian of both women, his bulky shoulders straight and expected scowl etched on that ever-stern face. A moment passed, filled with silent tension between the two men, and then Brandon stepped forward.

Brayden braced himself. *How could you do this? How dare you take this girl and break her? This isn't what Murphy men do!* He expected all that and more from this brother. What he did not expect was Brandon's arms suddenly surround his shoulders, dragging him into a hard hold.

Fists at his side, Brayden held statue still.

"I'm so sorry, brother." Brandon's hold didn't loosen as his voice came out deep and raw. As if he truly felt a portion of this agony and was willing to bear up for the brother who had scorned him.

What was he to do with this? Brayden felt his lips tremble. The steel shield he'd quickly lifted to take cover behind slipped away. Brandon's hold was unyielding, the refuge Brayden had longed for but didn't expect, and suddenly the tears he'd held hostage over the past several days found escape.

In that moment, there was no more animosity. No more resentment. There was only this heavy grief and this brother who offered to carry some of the weight on his own muscled shoulders. This moment would forever be etched on his heart. He'd forever recall the smell of Brandon's soap—likely Old Spice Timber, as Brandon was not a creature of change—as strong hands gripped his shoulders and held tight. The security of strength holding up his weakness. And the unexpected relief of having someone know what he'd wanted no one to discover, and that person, this brother, of all people, delivering compassion into his mess.

Grace gripping him in the hardest part of this jarring pain.

Brayden yielded to the relief of it, even if he knew it was a temporary thing.

_____ele_____

Audrey fiddled with a loose bit of yarn on the afghan she'd tossed over her legs. Megan sat next to her on the sofa, her body turned to face Audrey. On the low coffee table, twin mugs of mulled cider swirled steam upward, offering the rich scent of apples, cloves, and cinnamon. Megan's doing, clearly remembering how much Audrey loved hot apple cider when the cool nights of fall had come to relieve summer.

"I wish we'd known." With one elbow propped on the back of the seat, Megan leaned her head against her hand, and with the other, she covered

Audrey's knee. "Nothing would have kept me from being there with you. You know that, right?"

Sniffing, Audrey nodded. "I know. We just weren't ready to tell everyone yet." Her face burned at the unspoken reason for their silence about the baby. Megan knew, of that Audrey had suspected from the beginning, and she was nearly certain of it now.

"When was he due?" Nothing but gentleness existed in Megan's tone.

"Beginning of January." Twisting the yarn around her finger, Audrey swallowed and then glanced up at Megan.

Megan's hand moved from Audrey's knee and gently surrounded her fidgeting hands. "Audrey."

With an inhale for bravery, Audrey moved her chin up.

"Your parents will want to know."

Tears burned, but Audrey nodded.

"They love you."

Again, she nodded.

"Please tell them. Let them into this grieving. They would have loved this little boy." Megan tugged on Audrey's hand, and Audrey willingly leaned into Megan's shoulder, sagging into the comfort offered.

"I hope so."

"Know it, Audrey. Do not doubt it for a moment." Both arms surrounded her now, and Megan sighed. "Oh, how I have missed you, my friend. So much."

How could Audrey have any more tears left to leak? Yet more sprung forth. "I've missed you too."

"This cannot remain standard. This distance between us. If our friendship could survive me being a preening brat, then surely we can survive you getting married and moving away."

It was more than that, wasn't it? Audrey had been headstrong and rebellious. A disappointment. And ugly at times, particularly when Megan had tried to make her see exactly the path Audrey had been treading.

"What's more . . ." Megan had gained steamed and plunged forward, fingering the curls at the back of Audrey's head as she spoke. "This whole elope and then move away without a party thing is quite simply unacceptable. I'm throwing you a reception."

Audrey sat up. "Oh, Meg, please let's not talk about this. I can barely handle more than sipping my cider right now."

With a bend of her head, Megan molded a sympathetic pout. "Of course, sweetie. Now isn't the time. But you have warning. Tuck it away for when you are ready. It will happen, and when it does, you'll see how much you are loved."

Loved . . .

Without permission, Audrey's mind switched to Brayden. There was not much she wanted more in the world than his love. Perhaps, at that moment, her baby in her arms. But beyond that, Brayden's heart had been her whole desire. Her hope and prayer since the day she'd exchanged vows with him. Now, only four months into a rushed marriage done to cover up a whirlwind romance gone too far too fast, and after the loss of their baby—the reason he'd married her at all—Audrey felt that slim hope dim further. Perhaps even snuff out completely.

She couldn't win his heart. Now Brayden was stuck with her. Perhaps this marriage was to only give birth to resentment—that of her husband's. The thought caused her to suck in a sharp breath. She couldn't live with that.

Megan sat up straight, regripped Audrey's hand. "You okay?"

"Fine." Audrey raked teeth over her bottom lip. "I'm fine." So many lies spoken. How many more would Audrey add? She wasn't fine. She and Brayden weren't fine. And everything was not going to be okay.

ele

"Can you take any time off at all?" Brandon meandered beside Brayden as the brothers strolled beside the lake.

The lowering sun kissed the western sky with muted pinks and soft oranges—the golden hour, Mom would call it. September's cooler evening breath danced off the waters, tagging the splash of the fountain in the lake's belly, before it touched Brayden's neck and face, offering a chilled balm. Inhaling a long draw, a touch of moisture mixed with the usual tinge of dust and, now, fall leaves.

A sense of surreal existence struck Brayden as he took in what was technically beauty surrounding him. An evening such as this, he should be out for a walk with his wife. He'd slide his hand around hers, and she would lace her fingers in his. They'd pause, turn to face the western display of color hovering above the silhouette of mountains. Audrey would inhale, as he'd just done, and then she'd smile. Perhaps lean into his shoulder, her head resting on his arm.

With all of his heart, he wanted that to be this scene, this moment. Sadly, it wasn't. Perhaps sadder still, that scene hadn't played out more than three times in their marriage. Three times. In four months. Could he really not have spared thirty minutes for evening strolls with his wife? Thirty minutes to hear how her day was, how she was feeling, discover the layers of who she really was?

Did he really know Audrey?

The ache gripping his chest twisted, driving all his failures deeper.

"Brayden?" Brandon stopped, causing Brayden to cease the autopilot shuffling of his feet. "Are you with me here?"

Clearing his throat, Brayden rubbed his neck. "There's never enough time. You know?" He scowled as he fixed his look on one of the swans as it glided over the rippling waters into a splash of orange light reflected from a lamp. "There's always something to chase."

"Stop chasing then."

Brayden jerked his gaze to Brandon. "I'll never catch up if I do that."

"Catch up to what?"

"You." The answer dropped from his tongue without consideration. But there it was.

"Me?"

"You. Tyler. Jackson. Jacob. Connor. Matt."

"What are you talking about?"

"I can't." He shook his head, jammed his hands into his pockets, and with slumped shoulders, faced the movement of the swan again.

"Can't what?"

"I'm the youngest of a line of giants. I can't be you. Any of you. I can't uphold the Murphy standard. I've messed everything up, and now Audrey is paying for it. I can't go home. I can't face my wife. I can't even look at myself in the mirror."

A span of silence drifted from his brother, who stood straight and broad and tall as ever. Brayden braced himself for Brandon's crossed arms, for his stern frown, for the lecture sure to come. *Man up. Take responsibility. Fix your own problems.*

A year ago, all Brayden had wanted was everything his brothers had. The life of storied romance, everlasting love, and the respect of everyone around them. *Those Murphy boys, such men of honor. Kevin and Helen should be proud.* Words spoken of them. Not him. But soon, he'd thought, everyone would know his life had turned out swell too. It had been his due. That had been his belief. And so he took what he'd wanted, expecting his story to work out just fine, like his brothers' before him. After all, Jackson had been drunk when he'd married a stranger. Tyler had gone to rehab for opioid addiction. And Brandon, though often intolerable, had won the love of a beautiful heiress by way of agreeing to the dumbest arrangement ever.

It all had worked out. Why shouldn't Brayden's life?

He knew the contradiction of his thoughts. His brothers were all good men. Better men than he. Yet he felt he should simply *have* the life they'd found. If Brayden, in his twisted-up heart and mind, could discern the paradox in his rationale, certainly Brandon saw the incongruity with perfect clarity. That was, as it always had been, Brandon's gift—to see the idiocy in Brayden's ways. And he'd call Brayden out on it.

Tension built in Brayden's shoulders before Brandon finally sighed. "Bray . . ."

Here it comes. Brayden's heart braced for impact.

"We all fall on our face. Why else would men need a Redeemer?" Brandon held a firm grip on Brayden's shoulder. "You can always go home."

Fighting to keep a placid expression, Brayden writhed as the words penetrated deep, passing through the layers of his justifications, his guilt, and then his utter defeat. Not the arrow he'd shielded against. But the one that hit dead center.

Home. Though Brandon likely meant Sugar Pine and to their parents, that was not the meaning Brayden's heart turned toward.

Home.

He'd tried so hard to make things right with Audrey. To make their marriage what he wanted it to be—and surely that was a good thing. But perhaps there was Another he needed to make things right with first.

One who knew all the selfishness. All the ugliness. And now, all the agony gathered within. One with whom Brayden hadn't been right with in a long time.

Chapter Seventeen

(IN WHICH SORROW MAKES EVERYTHING MUDDLED)

Hours of prayer followed the weekend visit paid by his brother and sister-in-law. Prayer that had been long overdue. A bending of Brayden's heart was the working result of Brandon's intrusion into Brayden's deepest pain, and a forging product of the prayer that followed his older brother's visit.

Brandon had proven to be the unexpected anchor Brayden had needed in his stormy life, which, upon reflection, Brayden should have expected. Brandon was firm in conviction, and often that looked like overdone sternness. Maybe even self-righteousness. But along with Brandon's conviction to do well, to live well, to do what God would want him to do—a conviction he carried for himself, and maybe to his detriment, for others—there was an equal conviction to cling to mercy.

Because that was also as God would have him live.

Again, Brayden felt he had been born to and lived among giants. But this time he battled back the temptation to resent, to wallow in self-pity, and to revolt against expectations he'd believed were heavy and hard upon him. Instead, he appealed to God's grace.

As he pleaded with the One who sat upon heaven's throne for the redeeming that Brandon had spoken of, Brayden felt a new shape forming within. That asking for grace upon grace, mercy upon mercy, must have been smiled on by heaven. Suddenly Brayden no longer determined to be exactly the opposite of his stern and boring brother. Unexpectedly, his prayers had morphed into something that went strikingly like, *Lord, make*

me more like Brandon. Help me to want what you want. To live like You want
me to live.

Lord, help me to love my wife as I should.

There was the key, the missing part in Brayden's pursuit to make his
marriage work. Lessons long-ago impressed upon his young heart resurfaced, taught by a father and mother who had raised up those Murphy
giants. *Greater love has no one than this: to lay one's life down for one's*
friends.

Brayden had sought a life that was all selfish ambition and pride. Hadn't
that been why he'd pursued Audrey in the first place? Her quick adoration
had smothered the wound of Leah's betrayal and rejection. Her continued
devotion had stroked his arrogance. Her undeterred love, simply put, made
him feel good. He'd married her as a cover-up for sins he'd not wanted his
family to know about. His enjoyment of their marriage had been all about
pleasure and convenience.

Audrey loved. Brayden leeched. While that conviction was sickening
and hard to bear, facing the truth held a surprising hope of freedom.

Brayden continued to lift this new heartfelt plea. *Show me how love to my*
wife as I should. As Christ loved His church. He hoped, desperately and with
all his heart, that the work of Christ would bring forth a miracle in him—in
them—especially as Audrey seemed to slip deeper into what Brayden could
only diagnose as postpartum depression, made so much worse by the grief
that made them both ache.

Lord, help me to love her in this. To know how to walk with her through it.
And please, let me not be too late.

A walk. He remembered how he'd wished it'd been Audrey at his side
when it had been Brandon. How he'd lamented that he hadn't tried, hadn't
found the time to simply take her hand to go on a walk.

A walk, then.

He found her curled up on the sofa in the living room, the thick afghan she often used now swaddling her body, and her fists tucked under her chin. By the furrow of her brow, if she slept, it wasn't well.

Brayden lowered to the edge of the cushion, placing a hand on her hip. "Audrey?" he whispered.

She stirred but didn't open her eyes. "What?"

"I was thinking about walking to the lake."

"Okay." She tucked her chin down and gripped her blanket.

He moved his touch to her shoulder. "I mean, I was wondering if you wanted to go for a walk with me?"

"Not really."

Should he push her? She hadn't left the apartment in days—not since Megan and Brandon had gone home. Though a lump of doubt bulged his chest, Brayden leaned nearer, reaching to smooth back the wild strawberry curls. "Audrey, I think you need some fresh air."

She eyed him through squinted lids.

With the pad of his thumb, he traced the curve of her face. "Come for a walk with me, hon. Please?"

She didn't smile, nor did she speak an agreement. But she tossed her cover aside and put her socked feet to the floor. In the minutes that it took for her to retrieve her shoes and apply them to her feet, Brayden prayed again.

A cool evening breeze came off the mountains in the distance, greeting them as they turned from the parking lot onto the sidewalk that would lead them toward campus. Tentatively Brayden took Audrey's hand, and while silence stretched taut between them, he led her past the medical center and toward the lake on the opposite end.

"It was good of Brandon and Megan to come." Brayden nearly whispered, feeling young and insecure as he put effort to making bridges with his wife. "Was it good to spend some time with Megan?"

Audrey's arm hung limp at her side, her hand cold and lifeless in his palm. "It was kind of them to come." Her voice was strained, and her words sounded cautious.

Her lifelessness scared him. The distance she continued to put between her heart and his pulsed panic in his veins even as it made his chest painfully constrict. If only he'd been the husband he should have from the start. If only he'd loved. Perhaps then they'd have a foundation that wouldn't be crumbling faster than he could rebuild it. If he'd not been so blindly selfish, maybe his wife would trust him to hold tenderly her shattered heart.

Instead, she shielded it. From the world, but most painfully, from him. *God, let me not be too late!*

Near the lake, he paused beside a large boulder and tugged her to a stop. He had to nudge her to turn toward him. He sighed, sending that desperate plea silently to the only One he could imagine had the power to undo the damage Brayden had done, and to rebuild what should have been done right in the first place. Rubbing the back of his neck, he finally found the courage to look down, to tip Audrey's chin up with gentle fingers, and to take the full impact of her sad green eyes. So much sorrow, he could hardly recognize the woman in front of him as the girl he'd married only a few months before.

Gone was the young woman who'd hummed happily while she rolled out dough for a pie. The joyful, hopeful girl who had washed his clothes, come to him with proud delight when he'd passed his exams, who had given herself wholly to him, heart and body. She had collapsed into the broken shell who held him at a distrustful distance. All because he'd been reckless. All because he'd been arrogant and selfish.

This was how he'd been to her, who he'd proven himself, even while she'd loved him steadily. Brayden felt naked and ashamed as he stared into the damage he'd forged.

Swallowing, he forced himself to speak what he didn't want to say. "You thought I would be angry, didn't you?"

Audrey searched the ground, as if she'd lost something there. She moistened her lips twice, and he caught the quiver in them. As pain pierced his heart yet again, he pulled her hand up to his chest cradled it close. "This isn't a setup for an argument. It's not a trap. What it is, is me trying to find a way to tell you that I was wrong. I shouldn't have tried to hide the baby. I shouldn't have tried to cover up my failures, and I shouldn't have kept you from telling your friends and family."

Audrey lifted a shoulder, a gesture that was weak and unconvincing. "It doesn't matter now, does it?"

The emotion strained against his throat so tight that Brayden could barely make words come out. He managed only two. "It matters."

It mattered because this wasn't all he wanted her to know of him. That he was spoiled and controlling. And so pathetically weak that he couldn't own his failures to his family or to hers. It mattered because that wasn't who he wanted to be.

Brayden couldn't form the words to tell her all of that. It seemed he could barely breathe for the weight of all that was wrong in that moment. All he could do was pull her in close and wrap a tight hold around this woman who was slipping away.

She let him. Even leaned against him.

Lifeless.

God, let me not be too late.

The request grew more desperate every time it was repeated. Because the fear that he was loomed larger with each breath.

Audrey had offered him her heart from the beginning. That should have been the gift he'd treasured most in his life. How tragic that he only realized that fact after what she'd given so freely had been crushed.

·___ℯ ℓ ℓ___

Sleep, come.

Audrey curled into a ball, one shoulder pressed into the mattress and the seaside-honeymoon quilt pulled up to her ears. Squeezing her eyes shut, she demanded her memory not reframe moments of that weekend. Had it only been months ago? Seemed like another life. Against her will, moments she'd savored of that first weekend as Mrs. Audrey Murphy resurfaced. Brayden had promised, insisted all would work out. It would be okay. Those were his words. She'd drunk them in, swallowed such tales deep as they'd stood on the beach that first day. The day she'd determined to make him happy, because then, if she did, he'd love her. The way she loved him.

What a foolish girl she'd been to cling to such a flimsy promise made by a man who had only done so to smooth out the life he'd wrinkled. How could everything work out, be okay? She and Brayden had plunged headlong into a romance that she'd known wasn't healthy. She'd been warned the path she'd begun with Brandon's reckless little brother wasn't a good one. How had she expected that all would be well when they'd both spurned good advice and sound warnings? When they'd charged forward with reckless passion, and then when boundaries had been broken and consequences made known, they'd opted to cover up mistakes.

They'd done all this? No. Brayden had led the way. In selfishness and with manipulation, not tenderness. Not love.

Bitterness stirred foul in her gut.

But what of now? The quiet, meek question drifted into the stormy thoughts, and though Audrey wanted to silence it so that she might drift to sleep with her cut and bleeding heart under the guard of anger, she couldn't ignore the gentle probe.

What of now, what of that very evening? Her husband had taken the night off from studying, had led her gently into an evening walk that only weeks ago Audrey would have thought lovely and even romantic. He'd spoken to her tenderly, with humility. Then held her close. Been an offer of strength in her weakness.

What of all that? Signs of love, though he'd never once spoken of it? A steadiness of heart that, though she'd looked for it before, had not made itself known until now?

Or something else?

Something else, the bitterness within her seethed. *You keep searching for love from a man who only knows how to take that precious thing, not give it.*

But it seemed . . .

No. *Guilt. Just like the day you told him about the baby. Guilt, not love.*

Audrey winced as those harsh thoughts sank like a stake into her heart. The mattress at her back shifted by the weight of her husband. He settled into the space, adjusting the covers, and then stilled.

A dichotomy of longings stretched her in two directions as he lay beside her unmoving. She didn't want his touch, not if it was driven by guilt, and that only because his pride had taken an arrow. Oh, but she did . . . Those arms that had held her beside the lake, they had promised to hold her while she grieved. A tender vow of his faithfulness and care that she'd ached for since the moment she'd discovered she was pregnant. One that hinted there would be hope and life after this storm.

Longing for that comfort battled the resentment of the lie she felt certain was in that silent promise. Which would win, hope or resentment?

No clear answer presented itself before Brayden rolled onto his side and laid a gentle hand on her hip. "Audrey?" he whispered.

She sniffed and then swallowed. "I'm tired, Brayden."

"I know." He shifted near, until his chest touched her back, and then he curved his arm around her in a hold that felt protective and tender.

What of this? A tear seeped from the corner of her eye as she held herself stiff.

"I am here." The warmth of his breath spilled onto her cheek and ear as he whispered the words, as if a promise.

Could she trust such a promise from him? Trust this subtle offer of the heart she'd so longed for these past months?

No!

Audrey clapped her mind shut against that angry response. As Brayden's thumb smoothed soft circles onto her bare shoulder, her taut muscles unfurled. He moved once more, this time to cradle her in both arms.

She sank into him. Then slept deeply.

Weeks crawled by, and late September bled into mid-October. The burnt oranges and sharp crimsons of the maples dotting campus turned crispy after a few hard frosts, and then they vacated their branches, scattering with increased numbers along the pathways. Brayden continued his efforts toward being a better man, a better husband. He texted Audrey with more regularity, made room for an evening walk in his study schedule at least once a week, and curled his body around hers at night.

It seemed there was progress, though slow it may be. She responded to his texts with more than single-word replies. Seemed to anticipate his suggestion for walks with less hesitancy. Sank against him more immediately when he put his arms around her at night.

But still she held out, kept a barricade around the heart she'd previously offered to him without reserve. She grieved privately, maintained the shield she'd positioned after their baby died, and didn't seek him as she used to. And her smile . . . That had become nearly extinct.

Her withdrawal hurt. So much more than he'd anticipated. Had this been what she'd felt all these months when she'd offered him her heart and he'd taken it without stretching out his for her taking? If so, was this revenge? That seemed too cruel for his young wife—she wasn't wired with selfish spite.

Then the block between them was likely the lingering grief and depression.

Patience, then. Not a tool well practiced in Brayden's hands. Some days came to an end with buckets of frustration. Would there be sunnier skies on the other side of these cloudy days? Could he summon them to come sooner?

Such thoughts possessed his mind as he shouldered his school pack and exited the medical lab. He should have been focused on the lab he'd just completed, committing the information to memory. There would be a written exam in which he'd have to detail the process and consequences of mosquito-borne diseases at the end of the week. Even so, Brayden couldn't train his mind on anything but Audrey.

"You never used to scowl this much." A bump against his arm followed Leah's teasing voice.

Brayden looked down and didn't bother fixing a welcoming expression on his face. "Lots on my mind."

"How about you unload some of it on me over a cup of coffee?"

"Not today, Leah." He'd avoided her for a couple of weeks, careful to stay in classrooms and labs extra long and away from the union as much as possible. Today he'd not been as vigilant.

Leah latched her hand on his elbow. "You've been missing. Now you're upset. What's going on?"

"I told you, lots on my mind."

Large blue eyes searched him as Leah tugged him to a stop. "Bray. We're friends. Talk to me."

Her concern seemed genuine, and suddenly it was like the exhaustion of his beaten heart found a moment of rest. Drawing in a breath, Brayden allowed himself a moment when the complexity and hardness of life eased.

Leah tipped her head. "It's not all roses and sonnets, is it?"

"Marriage?"

She nodded and sighed. Then her hand slid from his elbow to his bicep, and she led him toward the less traveled side of the stadium that would take them to the union.

Warning flared fresh. Brayden extricated his arm from Leah's hold and opened space between them. "I can't."

"Can't what?"

"Look." He jammed fingers into his hair. "Things are . . ."

"Difficult right now?" Leah spoke into his pause. "I get it. I already told you that things with Aiden and me aren't always happy."

"It's not what you think."

"Then what is it?"

Brayden ground his back teeth, attempting to lock away the emotion building up rapidly in his chest. "My wife was pregnant. She—we lost the baby a few weeks ago."

Those beautiful blue eyes widened, and Leah's expression became all sympathy. "Oh Brayden. I'm so sorry. You didn't say before."

He pinched the bridge of his nose then nodded. "We hadn't told anyone yet."

The touch of her hand on his was barely a warning before she slid both arms around his waist. Brayden froze, keenly aware of her comfortable familiarity—her scent that was ginger and oranges, the silk of her glossy blond hair now brushing his bare arm. He'd held this girl countless times, and she'd held him.

This is dangerous.

Even so, here was comfort. A place of rest for his tangled mind, his frayed emotions—one he hadn't found at home, with Audrey.

Audrey.

Brayden squeezed his eyes shut as the thought of his wife pricked gut-deep pain. He curled around it. Physically, he curved around the one holding him that moment, his arms circling the one he'd once thought to marry. Clinging to the one who was *not* now his wife. Just for this moment, for this breath of comfort so that he could regain a bit of strengt.

Leah stepped in closer, the planes of her body pressing into his as the circle of her arms tightened.

Danger!

This time Brayden came awake, snapped out of the fog created by loneliness, frustration, and ache. His arms unlatched as if his skin burned, and he stepped back, putting a wide gap between them.

"Bray—"

He held up a hand. "Please don't, Leah. If Audrey—"

"We're friends. Surely your wife can accept that you have a close female friend."

"My wife is an emotional mess right now." Brayden swallowed and then forced a serious, hard look on Leah. "And to be honest, I think you are too."

"Me?" Her tone finished the rest of her unspoken thought. *She* wasn't the one getting things confused in her head—her heart.

He was a mess.

His thoughts wouldn't go where he needed them to go. His emotions were as treacherous as cancer. He felt wrung out and flattened, and he desperately wanted a moment of reprieve. A safe place to breathe for just a minute. A friend, a trusted soul to confide in, one who would offer real compassion that didn't totter on the edge of disaster.

That couldn't be Leah. If not because of her, because of him.

"Brayden, you're clearly not okay."

Rubbing his neck, he refused to allow himself to meet her eyes, knowing he was too weak not to take whatever he found there and twist it into what he wanted it to be. "Like I said, it's been a rough couple of weeks."

"Let me help."

He shook his head. "You can't."

"I'm your friend." Her hand stretched across the space still between them, the light touch of her fingers landing on the back of his hand.

Brayden shot a prayer heavenward for resolve and then dared to meet her look. "Thank you for that." He took a light hold of her hand on his and then gently moved it away. "But not this. If friendship is your true offer, then give me space." A moment throbbed hard, and Brayden swallowed. "Let me go, Leah."

At the hurt-filled furrow of her brow, he turned away, forcing his strides the opposite direction.

God, I want to be the husband my wife needs. His vision blurred as liquid heat glazed his eyes. Brandon had been right last year when he'd called Brayden selfish and weak. He'd been right to demand that he leave Audrey alone. Brayden wanted now, more than ever, to do exactly what Brandon had charged him to do: to be the man he'd wanted everyone to believe he was.

Never had he seen the truth so clearly: he wasn't that man.

Please help.

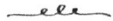

The day had been long and awful. Through it, the brokenness of his life continued to rub his soul raw. Like a slow drip on a leaky faucet, two words trickled from his heart and mind: *Please help. Please help.* Help his marriage. Help his wife. Help him. The last, most of all—help him be a better man.

In the cool evening, as a rare storm gathered over the mountains and billowed in the gray dusk, Brayden decided to try. He sat straight from his slumped-over-a-text position at the table and aimed his attention toward Audrey, who studied on the sofa.

"I think it's time you teach me your magic."

Her head came up, puzzled expression pinning on him. "My magic?"

Brayden tossed the pen he'd been fidgeting with to the table. "Yes. With pies." He stood, clapping his palms together in anticipation.

Eyelids pinching, Audrey heaved a reluctant sigh.

Not the responses he'd hoped for. Still, he was a persistent man who had been starved of his wife's smile. He strode to the sofa and gathered her hands in his.

Audrey stood as he tugged. "You want me to make a pie?"

"No, I want you to teach me how you make your pies."

Still no smile. No light flickered in her eyes. She simply followed him as he led her to the kitchen, one hand tucked in his. "The dough has to chill."

"Okay." He dipped a nod.

Her mouth scrunched to one side, and her shoulders moved with a slow breath. "What kind?"

"Whatever you want."

"I don't want pie, Brayden."

He blinked, nearly ready to give in to defeat. Instead, he shrugged, fighting to maintain a light tone. "We can give it to a neighbor."

Audrey searched his gaze, the depths of her green eyes revealing confusion and distrust. Finally, her brows folded inward. "Why are you doing this?"

His chest tightened, and the breath he drew was ragged. As emotion swelled his throat, making words hard to squeeze out, he lifted a hand and curved his palm around her jaw. He ran his thumb alongside the corner of her mouth and finally forced the words free. "I am desperate for your smile."

Her lids slipped closed, but beneath her lashes, he could see the gathering of moisture. "I'm not sure I have one anymore," she whispered.

Heart splintering yet again, Brayden palmed the back of her head, his fingers tangling into the mass of untamed curls, and drew her in close. When she pressed her forehead into his shoulder willingly, he knew a measure of relief. Pressing a kiss to her hair, he wrapped her in a secure hold. "It's okay," he murmured into her hair. "I'll take this instead."

For the first time in weeks, Audrey lifted her arms, anchored her hands near his shoulder blades, and held him in return.

Find comfort here. He did, molding around her like a protective cocoon, savoring the feel of *this* woman in his arms.

Progress. Small, slow, hard progress. But progress nonetheless. Brayden pressed her in close and breathed her scent—a clean blend of something floral and bright. The fragrance Megan had given her—sweet peas, was it? He angled his face and tucked into her neck. Yes, sweet peas and a subtle trace of vanilla.

"I can't find my way out of this darkness." Her husky confession surprised him, and the response in his chest was both a painful splitting and a lifting hope. He hated seeing her writhe this way, but that she would say such a thing to him . . .

There was progress in that.

"Time." He ran a palm down her spine and then back up, stopping at her shoulder. The single word echoed in his mind. *Time.* What he hadn't been willing to endure before. Time for life to unfold. For wounds to heal. For love to grow.

Could it be that God would take this hard place and use it to build something firmer, something resilient where Brayden had only laid a flimsy layer of his own selfish design?

Yes, God could do that. There seemed an inkling in Brayden's mind, in fact, that He would. A whisper of a conditional promise. The qualification pressed upon Brayden? *Time.*

God, let it be so. And help him to be both patient and strong.

Audrey lifted her face from her hiding place against his chest and searched his face with a sad, weary green gaze. "How long?"

There seemed to be layers in those two words. How long before she would be released from this dreary bleakness? He didn't know. How long would he be patient with her, as he hadn't been before?

The challenge issued not only by her, but by heaven.

He bent and feathered light kisses on the moist corners of her eyes. "As long as it takes."

Chapter Eighteen

(IN WHICH THE TRUTH ISN'T CLEAR)

The calendar turned over another page, and Audrey sipped on the cooler November air, stirred with crips brown leaves on the ground and a mild hint of snow that drifted off the nearby mountains. As she made an intentional effort to savor the taste, she dared to take in a touch of hope.

Time. That had been Brayden's hoarse prescription to her darkness, whispered two weeks before. As he'd held her in the kitchen that evening, and for the first time since the loss, she'd clung to him in response, had dared to believe that he'd not only give her all the time she needed, but also that on the other side of this thick fog, he would remain this new, tender, attentive man he'd recently become. She'd allowed the sprouting of a seedling of hope that his heart had moved toward her.

Time would indeed tell.

She yearned to discover what would be true, and she feared it at the same time. Brayden had always possessed the ability to work consideration into their interactions. It was part of his irresistible charm. But, as she'd bitterly realized in the darkest moments of retrospection, doing so typically had an angle fueling the actions. Something he wanted for himself. It had been manipulation, not love, directing the displays of kindness.

In the moments of these hostile thoughts, her mind most often traveled to that day beside the river when he'd proposed the second time, persuading her with kisses and sweet words to follow him over the cliff that had led them where they were now: not only grieving the loss of the baby, but wondering if this marriage had any substance at all. Not once in that scene had Brayden declared his love. His angle had been a cover-up.

Just a cover-up.

Such realizations made it difficult to embrace this new side of her husband, even with as much as she wanted to. Audrey was hesitant—no, terrified—to believe that what Brayden did now in all his gentle attention had much to do with her heart at all.

Even so, she longed for what seemed farfetched to be revealed as truth. So there she lived, caught in the tension of fear and hope. If he proved genuine, they had a real chance at making it together.

If he proved false?

Her heart would be twice broken. Audrey could barley breathe for the first shattering. How could she survive the second?

Sitting on a bench beneath a fall-stripped maple, she clutched her laptop and biology textbook tight against her clenching chest. Staring across the lot toward the bulge of mountains in the distance, but not really seeing, she searched for the means to sweep such gloomy things from her mind. How was she ever going to escape these clouds if more kept crowding in? Somehow, she needed to get a grip on her inner world, to direct her thoughts toward things that were helpful and good. Wasn't that what the Bible said to do? To think on things that were excellent and praiseworthy?

What exactly did that verse prescribe?

Audrey took up her smartphone and opened a new search. Ah, in Philippians. Chapter 4, verse 8. "Whatever is true, whatever is noble, whatever is right, whatever is pure, whatever is lovely, whatever is admirable—if anything is excellent or praiseworthy—think about such things."

Squeezing her eyes shut, she focused on scattering the cluttered thoughts plaguing her mind and replacing them with the apostle Paul's instructions.

"Audrey?" Victoria's concerned voice intruded on Audrey's practice. "You okay?"

Blinking, Audrey looked at her friend as she lowered onto the seat beside her. "I'm okay."

Victoria shook her head. But rather than push for the truth, she gripped Audrey's hand. "Buy you lunch?"

She wasn't hungry. Hadn't been particularly hungry in weeks, which might explain the way her clothes hung from her frame as if she were a little girl who had raided her mother's closet.

"Come on." Vitoria firmed her grip and tugged, obviously sensing Audrey's unvoiced rejection of her offer. "Fries. Who can resist fries? And ice cream. You can dip those salty suckers in a pure frozen vanilla, and I promise, one won't be enough."

Lifting a wisp of a smile at Victoria's efforts, Audrey agreed with a mild nod. "Okay."

Though November, the clear sky allowed the bright sun to warm their path. Victoria chatted about the biology test she was sure she'd just bombed and then pointed out the pair of swans as they glided over the rippling lake in the distance. "Don't you love that the school has adopted them?"

Audrey hadn't given much thought to it. "It is sweet."

Victoria squeezed against Audrey's shoulder and then turned toward the union. Audrey followed compliantly, nodding here and there as Victoria found more of not much to comment about. Bless her efforts, her friend was working hard to help. As much as it didn't seem helpful, the effort was kind.

Something admirable. That was what that was, and Audrey made an intentional note of it, just as the verse in Philippians had instructed.

They passed through the doors, and Victoria made a straight line to her favorite fast-food vendor. Once there, she paused her chatter for a moment, and Audrey was able to focus her thoughts on the verse. *Anything excellent or praiseworthy* . . . Perhaps if she made a more concentrated effort in this, she would not remain chained in the darkness quite so long.

Victoria's attention drifted over the students scattered throughout the union, her eyes landing on someone in particular, and she sighed. "Oh, she would be stunning," she mumbled.

"Who?" Audrey turned to find whoever had deflated her bubbly friend's countenance.

Victoria directed Audrey's search to a table in the far corner. "The blonde."

Audrey followed Victoria's flicked gesture, and then her breath stalled. Brayden.

Her heart clenched with cruel severity.

"We first-year nurses all crushed on that guy spring semester, and who could blame us. That dark hair and mischievous set on his mouth. Like a brown-eyed Neil Caffrey." Victoria carried on with her dramatics, oblivious to Audrey's held breath.

Audrey fought to calm the raging hot pulse thundering through her body, to regain a grip on her buck-wild thoughts now exploding. "Neil Caffrey isn't real."

"Matt Bomer is."

"True, but he's married." *Married* clanged in Audrey's head. She tried desperately to distract herself from everything falling to pieces inside of her with the current conversation.

Victoria shrugged. "I have eyes nonetheless. And we weren't drooling over Neil-Matt anyway." She nodded toward the couple in the distance and sighed dramatically. "Never mind the rumor that he had a girlfriend. A girl can hope. But then I heard that he got married. Of course, he *would* have married Barbie. It just figures, right?"

Audrey swallowed hard as she looked over the woman sitting across from her husband. She was gorgeous. Sleek, glossy blond hair hung perfectly straight past her shoulders, not a single strand of curly frizz to be seen. A stylish cashmere cardigan hung on her slender shoulders in a very Taylor

Swift vibe. And by her profile, her smile was warm and lovely and focused on the man sitting across from her.

On *Audrey's* husband.

Audrey's eyes moved back to Brayden, who listened attentively to the lovely woman gazing up at him as if he were her whole galaxy. Brayden appeared mesmerized.

Audrey's hands trembled. "How do you know that's his wife?"

"I see them eating together here at least once a week. And though she doesn't look it much, which isn't fair either, she's pregnant." Victoria heaved one last regretful breath and then turned away. "Oh well. There are other men out there, right?" She giggled. "Not that you're worried about it, my married friend. Some of us, however, suffer from empty-ring-finger syndrome." She lifted her left hand and wiggled her fingers. But then her eyes pinched, her hand dropped against her thigh, and she leaned closer to Audrey. "You okay? You're a little pale."

That was likely because Audrey thought she'd be sick right there in the middle of the union. She touched her forehead, finding it damp. "I'm not feeling the best."

"Likely because you never eat. Let me get you something with calories and protein in it."

Audrey barely registered anything Victoria said. Instead, she had looked back at the table, her gaze drawn to her husband as if he was her magnetic north.

No. He was her train wreck in motion. Happening now. Already the crash was collapsing her world. She wanted to fall into a sobbing, pathetic heap. She wanted to scream at the hot rending that was cruelly searing her chest.

She wanted to run and run and run.

His attention veered away from the beauty who had, up to that point, absorbed every ounce of his interest, his chin swerving toward Audrey. Eyes connected. Widened. Brow furrowed.

Time froze. The world stopped. In that shared gaze there was only him and her. Everything within her hardened, and she couldn't breathe. Then Brayden shook his head, as if he read her every thought, could see the ribbons he'd slashed into her soul. Audrey locked her jaw and swallowed, somehow obeying the command of her mind to withhold the stinging tears that gathered just below her lids. Just as Brayden scurried from his seat, Audrey severed their connection. She turned toward the exit and made her feet move.

Behind her, Victoria called her name. Audrey didn't respond, only broke through the door and scrambled down the concrete steps. Once on the path, her stride turned to a jog.

Her name cut through the November breeze again, this time set forth by Brayden's voice.

Ignoring it, Audrey ran.

─────ele─────

God, how could I be so stupid!

Brayden stopped at the bottom of the steps and watched as his wife broke into a full sprint. Should he chase her? Cause more of a scene than had already been stirred? He didn't much care what anyone thought, but it mattered how it would affect Audrey.

That moment, played out just seconds before, flashed anew in his mind. It'd been as if he could feel her eyes on him, and his heart had already plunged before he'd even turned to search her out. And indeed, there she was. Lips parted in horrified shock, Audrey stared at him with the destroyed look of one utterly betrayed. In his head, he'd actually heard the sound of shattering glass.

"Brayden . . ."

Still sitting across from her, he'd been vaguely aware of Leah speaking his name, and worse, had felt the brush of her fingertips on the back of his hand. At that, his chest had collapsed against a feeling that must be something close to what it must be like to take a gunshot. Hot, ripping pain burned clean through. Shaking his head because he knew *exactly* how this appeared to his wife, he'd jerked his hand from Leah's touch and scrambled to his feet, but Audrey had already given him her back.

She'd run, and she didn't look back.

What was he going to do?

"Brayden?"

He jolted toward the voice coming from behind him and immediately resented her following his path. More, resenting that she yet again distracted him from his purpose. "Leave me alone, Leah."

Hurt filled her expression, but she said nothing. Only held out his backpack by the top loop. Brayden grabbed it and turned back to search the path Audrey had taken.

Among the varied students wandering the campus pathway toward the medical center, no strawberry curls caught the shimmering oranges and yellows of this autumn sunshine. Audrey was gone.

Gone.

He'd lost her. The unmerciful fist gripping his heart squeezed harder, and Brayden found that it hurt to breathe.

"Your wife?" Leah said, her voice soft. Regretful, maybe?

"Yes." He fixed a glare on the blonde who dared to remain at his side. "My wife. You can imagine what she thinks."

Leah looked at her hand, now resting on her baby bump. "I . . ."

"I asked you before to leave me alone."

"I know, but we're—"

"Not friends, Leah. We've never been friends. All we ever were together was toxic."

Slowly her face lifted back to his, her eyes glazed. "That's not—"

"I'm not going to stand here and argue you with. I have a marriage that was already strained. Now it's been tossed on the rocks. This ends right here." He leaned in, his scowl pinching hard between his eyes. "Do you understand me?"

With a visible swallow, Leah let her lids close and then drew a shuddered breath. She nodded.

Brayden jammed the shoulder strap of his backpack over his arm and moved to go.

"Bray?"

"What," he barked, halting but not looking at her.

"I'm sorry."

He swallowed, not knowing what to say, and fearing that whatever he dared let slip from his tongue would be ugly. This was already a disaster—he already had more regret to wade through than he thought he could manage. Rather than muttering something he'd likely have to seek forgiveness for later, he pushed his stride forward. Away from Leah and toward his wife.

Please, help me fix this.

Beyond that desperate prayer, thoughts wouldn't form in his mind as he made his way home. Turned out, it wouldn't have mattered if he'd been able to piece together the perfect speech, a seamless apology.

Audrey wasn't there.

—ee—

She ignored over a dozen texts. All from Brayden.

Please, Audrey. We need to talk.

Where are you?

It's not what you think, I swear.

It's been over an hour, please say something.

I'm really worried about you, babe. Tell me where you are.

At least tell me you're okay.

Come home.

Talk to me.

On they went, begging her to go home. To let him explain.

Eventually, she'd have to go back to the apartment. At that point, she had nowhere else to go. But for now, as the sun sank behind the line of mountains to the west, she remained on the lonely bench overlooking the healing garden at the hospital. This path she had walked a few times since delivering her stillborn son. There was a memory garden at the beginning of this trail, nameplates attached to various planters, small sculptures, and a large angel statue at the center of the dedicated area. Among them, one read simply *Baby Boy Murphy*.

They hadn't even given him a name. What kind of people were they who were so entrenched in a mess of their own making that they couldn't even name their son?

God, I am lost.

How had she become turned upside so quickly? A year ago she had plans, a hope and a future all laid out before her. She was going to go to the coast and go to school and become an RN and do good in the world and make her parents proud. Her life would be quiet, but useful and good.

She would be happy.

Now? She was so *un*happy. So broken inside that she couldn't determine which direction to take the next step. How had she come to this?

Brayden.

At the single thought of his name, a quiet sob quaked her whole frame. The fire that flared within tempted her toward hate. She'd loved him, given up everything for him—her plans, the respect of her family. Even her best friend was distant from her, even though now Megan was her sister through marriage. How could love destroy everything?

Because he hadn't loved her in return. Never did. Clearly, he never would. There would always be . . .

She pictured the beautiful woman he'd been with. Had she been Leah? Intuition seethed *yes, that was Leah.* The one who would forever possess Brayden's heart. The reason Audrey would never have it for her own.

Think on things that are true . . .

She didn't know for a fact that it'd been Leah. Oh, but her gut declared it. But even if that woman had been another, she'd gained Brayden's attention. Apparently often, according to Victoria. This was why he'd acted distant on occasion and then followed that withdrawal with forced attention. It had been a pattern of betrayal and guilt. And Audrey had been pathetically blind. Stupidly hopeful that Brayden's heart was somehow miraculously turning toward her.

Love had made her a fool.

Audrey lifted the phone in her palm and looked over the texts Brayden had sent. Not a single apology in them. And never, not that night, or any other time before, a declaration of love on his part. Why did he continue with this? The only reason he'd married her in the first place was because of the baby. Now, there wasn't a baby.

Brayden had been set free.

No, not entirely. Perhaps there was an ounce of honor in him—he was, after all, a Murphy. *She* had not yet set him free.

At that thought, her chest thrashed. How could there be more pain to feel? How could she still, after all this, have such a care for him embedded so deeply that it caused her breathless ache to think of letting him go?

This love was unkind.

The sound of crushed rock underfoot startled her from her sad musings. For hours she'd sat on this secluded overlook, undisturbed. The healing garden was always quiet, the path to this overlook an uphill one that most hospital goers weren't going to tread.

Who came, as the hour darkened, uphill to her lonely perch?

Sighing, she clutched her phone as a knowing whispered in her heart. Or was that more stupid hope? She did not want it to be hope.

"Audrey." Her name on his breath came with a sound of relief.

She forbade her heart to grasp it with any sort of tender feeling. Instead, she glanced at him with indifference and turned to watch the last bits of orange tuck itself into the hills for the night. "You found me."

"I searched for the car with my phone. I was worried." His stride stopped beside her, and she expected him to lower onto the bench. Instead, his knees sank into the gravel at her feet. "Please, Audrey, give me a chance to explain."

Pressing her lips into a tight line, she forced her attention to his face. Oh, but he did contrition so well, with that sheen in those dark-brown eyes, the deep furrow of his brow. Even a slight quiver of his lips.

"Do not play me, Brayden."

He shook his head. "I have never played you."

"No? Not ever?"

Swallowing, he only held a steady gaze. Was that a denial? Anger thrust upward.

"Who is she?" Audrey spat.

His gaze faltered, dropping toward the ground. "Leah."

"I thought so."

"I didn't seek her out."

"How long have you been seeing her?"

"I haven't been *seeing* her."

"Victoria says she sees you with her often."

His face whipped back up. "That doesn't mean I've been seeing her."

Audrey leaned back, seeking however much space between them she could find. "How long, Brayden?"

His jaw tightened, and he rubbed the back of his neck. "She found me at the beginning of the school year. Said she'd transferred here because her *husband* was deployed, and she wanted to be somewhere where she would have a friend."

A derisive laugh came hard from Audrey's chest. "A friend? That's adorable, Brayden. You must think I'm an idiot."

The look he latched on her nearly untied all her knotted rage. She almost believed he felt the agony and remorse that masked his features, passed into his gaze. "I swear, Audrey." With both hands, he gripped her arms. "There is nothing going on between Leah and me. I wouldn't do that to you."

"There doesn't have to be something physical for there to be something going on." Swallowing hard, Audrey pushed his touch away.

He shook his head, his stare adamant. "It is not like that, I promise. She sought me out every time. I even tried to tell her to leave me alone, but—"

"Oh, you tried? Poor, helpless Brayden. It must be hard to be so irresistible. Tell me—does she know you're married?"

"I told her, yes."

"Well, then you're covered, right? Except, you never told me. Four months into the semester, and you never once mentioned that the woman you have been in love with since you were fifteen was in town, at school, and sharing meals with you behind my back. Why would that be?"

"Because I knew this would happen!" He motioned between them, his tone sharp.

"Of course this would happen, Brayden! But once again, you chose a cover-up over honesty."

As quickly as his defensive position had set on him, it vanished. His shoulders caved, look dropped toward the ground.

"You're a coward, Brayden Murphy."

A defeated nod moved his head.

"And you played me."

Once again, he lifted an agonized look to her, shaking his head. "I swear I didn't."

Oh, the traitorous part of her heart! It wanted to take that as the truth. Could she truly be that weak?

Lifting both hands, Brayden cautiously cupped her jaw in his palms. At the gentleness of his touch as he brushed both thumbs across her cheekbones, Audrey's lids fluttered shut.

Yes, I am that weak.

"I love you, Audrey."

His whispered words were a blade slicing her heart. She borrowed strength from the pain. Eyes flying open, Audrey gripped his wrists and pulled away from his hold. "Do *not* say that."

Alarm wrote across his face. "But—"

"Not now. Not like this."

His lips closed, and fingers rolled into his palms as she held his hands away. "Audrey—"

She shook her head and shoved him until he landed on his backside in the crushed rock. "That's something that's supposed to come from the depths of your heart, not spoken as a line of manipulation." Emotion swelled hard in her chest, preventing her from saying anything more.

Brayden scrambled up, reaching for her again, but Audrey shook her head. He stopped. For a moment there was only aching silence between them. She wiped her face with the heels of her palms.

"Please, Audrey . . ." There was pleading in his hoarse voice.

Once more she shook her head and stood. "I just want to go home."

___ele___

She let him drive her home. In the pulsing silence, Brayden scrambled through his mind for a way to make this right. There was nothing.

He did love her. Truly, he did. But he hadn't before, not at the beginning. Not like he should have. Not like she did him. And now . . .

He was losing her, and there was nothing he could do. Not one thing.

Chapter Nineteen

(IN WHICH THERE IS SILENCE)

The night was agonizingly long. Even after Brayden quietly exited the apartment a little after 3:30 a.m. to go to work, Audrey's exhaustion didn't yield to sleep. Scenes jumped from one to the next in her mind.

The first time she'd met Brayden. He'd been a confident flirt. Usually, she would have dismissed such behavior as arrogant and unappealing, save for two things. First, Brayden looked every bit like his attractive older brother, Brandon, who Audrey might have had a mild and silly crush on. And second, rather than aiming his flirtation at Megan, as every other guy on the planet would have done, Brayden had set his attention on her. The part of Audrey's heart that had forever shrank in the shadows thrown by Megan's beauty, wealth, and popularity had blossomed in that sunshine of his attention.

Later, was that evening by the river when things went too far. It'd been a perfect early spring day, and after working alongside Brandon for most of it, Brayden had texted Audrey, asking if she'd go fishing with him. Not the first time for that. Those evenings had always been fun. Brayden was an adventurer, and he loved to laugh. Going along with him had been bright spots in Audrey's weekends. But that evening, as the sun had lowered, allowing winter's chill back onto the land, Audrey had shivered. Brayden had drawn her close. One kiss led to many, and his touch that had warmed her clean through stoked a blaze that neither bothered to extinguish. A choice, a mistake that would forever change her life.

After that were his proposals. First, the public ones. Audrey had been jarred speechless and hadn't known what to do. How could she reject his offer right there in the middle of everyone? Then, by the river, where he'd persuaded her with kisses, breathlessly banishing her fears and doubts. One part of her had wanted this to be the perfect beginning notes to their own beautiful love song. The other part knew what had been made clear in the time that had followed—this wasn't a ballad. Their song clanged and crashed and then had fallen silent. Such was the music of deceit.

And more recently, the day they'd held the tiny body of their stillborn son. It had been one of the few moments in their marriage that Audrey knew with certainty that the emotion she saw in her husband was what he felt to the morrow of his bones. No deception. No cover-ups. If they shared only one thing real, it was the heartache of that horrible day. Brayden had loved his son. How tragic that in their marriage, that was the only certainty she had regarding his heart.

And finally, the afternoon she'd only just slipped from. The pain of it still throbbed, and sleep would not lend her a reprieve.

At six, Audrey finally gave up on the hope for rest and instead brewed a cup of orange-spiced tea. Steam curled from her mug, wafting the tangy scent of cloves and oranges. Having swaddled herself in her favorite afghan, Audrey cradled the warmth of the mug in her hands and inhaled, hoping the aroma would ease the dull ache in her head. As she sat in the silence, tired and gritty eyes closed, she focused on making her mind quiet. No more memories flickering. No more anger boiling. No more fearful panic about what to do next.

Just. Quiet.

In that space was room for the pain to settle, and it did. As if had worked into pure exhaustion, the agony that had been a thrashing beast surrendered to the quiet. Rather than stabbing, burning, slashing, it became a hollow ache, one not quite so monstrous. Not quite so threatening. And there, Audrey's mind cleared enough to pray. Just one word, but it was everything.

Help.

As a gentle darkness enveloped her, she set aside her untouched tea, curled into the softness of her blanket, and sank into the cushions of the sofa.

And, finally, blessedly, slept.

———ele———

Morning had dawned bright and clear, as if oblivious to the storm still howling in Brayden's world. Or worse, mocking it. Bone tired from so much emotion, from zero sleep, and from nearly six hours of manual labor already done by ten in the morning, Brayden pulled into the spot assigned to his apartment, set his gearshift in park, shut off the engine, and draped himself over the steering wheel.

He had no idea what would happen once he climbed those steps and passed into the apartment. Would Audrey sob? Yell at him? Hold up a stone-cold wall of silence? He deserved any one of those options, and worse.

Would she even be there? Audrey was a clever girl. Though between them they had only his vehicle, she could figure out how to leave. Leave, and never come back.

The very thought left him painfully breathless.

Tears rolled down his nose and dripped onto his soil-smeared jeans. How tragic was it that when he finally got his heart in the right place, had finally been able to say the words he'd refused to utter when he wasn't sure they were true, was the same moment Audrey would take them as poison?

And that was his fault. He *had* manipulated her in the past. She had every reason to believe that *I love you* from his lips were nothing more than words honed as a tool. Even if he did, in fact, feel them with devastating depth.

He'd done this. All of it.

"I can't fix this." Brayden squeezed his eyes shut as he uttered the truth of his despair to his empty car. He leaned back and tipped his face upward. "God, I can't fix this."

He'd spent most of his life contriving ways to get whatever it was he'd wanted at any given moment. Usually contriving to gain what he saw his older brothers had and he'd deemed were justly his as well. A later bedtime. That special dessert the other brother had earned. The chance to participate in activities at a much younger age than the others had been allowed. A storied romance. He'd manipulated and schemed.

Brayden had hidden shameful things and thought he could go on his merry way, gaining the life he'd wanted.

Nothing stayed hidden forever, did it? More, nothing was truly hidden from God.

What would have happened if he'd surrendered his desires to God long before this mess had become the utter disaster it was? When he'd found out Audrey was pregnant, what if he'd owned up to his mistakes openly, asked forgiveness of those his actions had hurt—Audrey, her parents, and his? Maybe he and Audrey would have figured something out without being isolated and sneaky. Maybe then, at the tragedy of their son's stillbirth, she wouldn't have felt so horribly alone. Perhaps the grip of depression that followed wouldn't have been quite so strong. And his own guilt? Perhaps it would have not been so paralyzing.

He had no way of knowing now.

Or, going back further. What if he'd waited to pursue the inkling of interest he'd honestly had in Audrey until his own heart had been turned right? Rather than using her to smother the sting of Leah's betrayal and rejection, what if he'd brought that anger and pain to someone who could help him work through it? Better yet, what if he'd had an honest and trusting relationship with God and had been able to surrender all of it to Him?

Again, no way of knowing.

Even so, he suspected strongly that *this* day wouldn't feel so awful. The sunshine wouldn't feel so harshly out of place, the bird songs throughout the early morning as he'd worked wouldn't have seemed a parody of his own darkness. Had he done any of those things better, Audrey wouldn't be somewhere, hopefully in their apartment, shattered. Instead, he'd go up there, find his wife enjoying her morning tea, kiss her good morning, and they would continue building a life on a solid foundation of trust.

Of pure love.

But there was no undoing what had been done. Life didn't come with one of those pink erasers he'd collected in elementary school. He didn't get to simply rub away mistakes until they were nothing but rubbery dust that he could blow off the page and then begin again.

So, that left him there. Alone in his car, tears rolling beside his nose, not knowing what to do.

Begin there.

The thought felt foreign and a little absurd. Begin where?

I don't know what to do, he silently nudged back.

Ah, was that it? Admitting he didn't know what to do, he couldn't fix this? Was that the place to begin?

Not quite all of it. From distant memories of his childhood came a story about a man named David who had done something really terrible, and a man named Nathan confronted him. David stopped trying to hide what he had done then, because obviously God knew. David had *sinned*, and God knew.

God knew *every* sin.

But in the Bible, David, this great sinner, was known as *the man after God's own heart.* How could that be? What made him so special if David was a sinner just like everyone? Just like Brayden?

Brayden couldn't pin down a certain answer, but his mind landed back on a thundering truth he'd ignored for the last year or more: *God knew every sin.* How foolish he'd been to try to cover up what he'd done. A quick marriage, their secret baby, rearranging Audrey's entire life, all to cover up an act he knew their families would be disappointed in. He'd not made anything better.

He'd made everything worse.

I don't know what to—

Before that thought completed its echo, the text chime on his phone sounded. Unreasonable as it was, Brayden reached for the device, hoping Audrey was the sender.

She was not. But Brandon was.

You are heavy in my thoughts today, Brayden. Is everything okay?

Yesterday Brayden would have typed off a quick *I'm fine, thanks.* With a strong dose of irritation, he would have lied to his brother, who had proven to be a much better man than Brayden had esteemed him. Perhaps God had prompted Brandon's thoughts toward him that day?

It went against his proud nature, but Brayden stretched toward something different as he typed into his phone.

No. Everything is not okay. Audrey and I are not okay. I made a mess. Now I don't know what to do.

He hit Send before he could talk himself out of it. Then, squeezing the phone in one palm, Brayden leaned back and shut his eyes.

I'm sorry, Father. I'm sorry for this mess I made. Please . . . His outpouring paused there. Please, what? What did he long for most from the God he'd been ignoring for far too long?

Forgive me, because I have sinned.

There was silence. Hard at first. And then, a softer quiet.

Opening his eyes, Brayden inhaled slowly. The sunshine streaming through his windshield didn't feel quite so harsh.

—*ele*—

A soft click reached through the heavy sleep that had finally claimed her mind. Pressing her cheek against the softness at her side, Audrey batted away the coming wakefulness. She didn't want to wake up. Even in the haze of rest, she knew that life beyond this blessed darkness wasn't pleasant, and she didn't want to reenter it just yet.

Against her wishes, her senses came more alive as the smells of fresh-cut grass, damp earth, and working man overtook the lingering memory of cloves and oranges. A presence made his impression near her, throwing a cool shadow on her shoulder as he blocked the sun's path coming from the window. Brayden. His name pricked the pain that had eased during her rest. Though preferring to ignore his presence, Audrey pulled her face away from the safety of that soft cushion and peeled her eyes open.

Tentatively, he reached a hand down toward her. Hesitantly, he fingered the mess of curls that had drifted over the side of her face. Gently, he smoothed them away from her skin. Then he lowered onto the table in front of the sofa, maintaining the light touch of his hand on the edge of her face.

Audrey froze, not trusting herself. After all that had happened, she found her heart and body were still spelled by the warmth of his caress. How could she still be this pliable? She dug around her heart for the anger that would be her protection, and it wasn't hard to find. There, in the middle of the brokenness, was the fire waiting to be stoked again. With a fortifying breath, Audrey moved her gaze to nail Brayden.

She had not prepared herself for the open wound she found staring back at her. The richness of his dark eyes held a depth she'd never seen, pried open for her full inspection as had never been allowed before. Did she dare believe that this was Brayden, her held-back husband, heart wide before her as he had never been?

Such a thought was a risk too costly to grasp.

Audrey eased back, pulling away from the tips of his fingers, the palm of his hand. His touch fell, hand retreated until it was paired with the other and folded as he pressed elbows to knees. Swallowing, his look darted to the floor, but only for a moment. He came back to her, as if forcing himself to remain unveiled for her inspection.

"Did you finally sleep?" he whispered.

Everything within tightened, making speaking difficult. Audrey nodded. "For a little bit."

"I'm sorry I woke you up."

She shrugged.

Silence. How could emptiness feel so heavy? How could the lack of words pierce as deeply as the ugliest insult? Her gaze fell to the looped yarn that occupied her fingers.

Across the short space between them, Brayden sniffed, and before she shot a glance to his face, he had moved. Once again, knees planted on the ground, he was in front of her. "I'm so sorry, Audrey. For everything. Every sin committed against you. Every kiss that was used as manipulation. Every way I twisted your affection for me to get my way. Regret isn't a strong enough word. I see all of it, and I hate it." Once more, his fingers wove into her hair, and he cradled her head with both hands. "I am sorry."

Mouth trembling, Audrey was afraid to move. "How can I believe you?"

"I don't know." He shook his head. "I've given you very little reason."

She thought on that, though much of her didn't want to. Had he given her reason to trust, despite all the reasons she had to distrust? These past

weeks, he'd been tenderly devoted. Patient with her while she wandered in
the darkness. Gentle and kind while she'd pulled away from him. And even
before that, had he been truly *un*kind?

He had not been.

And, had he lied last night? Could she really say that he'd used a declaration of love to manipulate her? He'd never said those words, though with
all her heart, she'd longed for him to. Had that been honor on his part?
Perhaps he would not say what he did not mean—not something like that.

Perhaps love was sacred to Brayden Murphy, as she'd always hoped it
would be.

The anger within wanted to dismiss such thoughts. In the past, Brayden
had manipulated. He had pushed and pried to get what he wanted.

Then again, was she all that different?

She'd wanted Brayden. Plain and simple. She'd ignored the counsel of
others, had strained the solid relationships she'd had with those who had
known her and loved her—and those who had known Brayden and loved
him too—to get what she wanted. Brandon and Megan, her parents, they
had warned both Brayden and Audrey that their sprinting relationship was
not wise. She and Brayden had *both* ignored such warnings. Worse, *she* had
resented the friends and family who would dare utter them.

As conviction plowed into her self-righteous rage, tossing water onto the
hottest of flames, Audrey forced herself to search the eyes that still held on
her.

Brayden's watch, fixed on her, was unshielded. Shame. Regret. Sorrow.
He let her see every broken piece. Even—what was that, down in the far
depths of that pool of open emotion?

Repentance.

An old-fashioned word. An old-fashioned concept.

Could Brayden Murphy even know what *repentance* was? Did Audrey?

To admit fault, be utterly broken over it, and to turn away from it. The notion was understood. But actually doing it?

Audrey felt as though she stood on a terrifying height, her toes peeping over the edge. There was so much to risk. Pride. Dignity. The shield of self-righteous anger. And most terrifying, the shredded bits of her heart, which surprisingly, still bent toward Brayden.

She squeezed her eyes shut, uncertain she possessed the courage to take that risk. "Did you mean it?" she whispered.

"With everything in me, Audrey. I can't say how sorry I am."

Blinking him into view again, she shook her head. "No." She swallowed. *Courage . . .* Would it matter? He would say what she would want to hear, wouldn't he? And even if he spoke truth, could it even begin to fix all that had fallen apart?

Oh, but she needed to know. "Yesterday—"

Brayden sucked in a breath as a flicker of desperate hope passed over his expression. Then he leaned forward, pressing his forehead to hers. "Yes." His voice cracked, and he brushed the curve of her cheekbones with both thumbs. "I love you, Audrey. Truly, with all my heart, my wife. I love you."

He gathered her close and held tight. Audrey laid her cheek on his shoulder and rested in his embrace. There wasn't a lie in his declaration. She knew it by the soul he allowed exposure in his gaze, by the emotion that wove deep in his husky voice.

Even so, the wounds throbbed. The risk still seemed too much, the shard pieces of them too many. Which left her muddled and confused.

He may be truly sorry, and there might be real love. But perhaps that wasn't enough to overcome all the broken pieces between them.

It might be too late for them, after all.

Chapter Twenty

(IN WHICH THERE IS TIME AND PERSPECTIVE)

For the first time, Brayden felt the true weight of privilege it was to have Audrey Smith Murphy in his arms. This sweet, smart, lovely young woman had trusted him, yielded to him, taken his name. How had he been so selfish, so idiotic, to have taken that lightly? Why had it required the blackest moment of his life to spill light on what a gift she was to him?

The only answer he had was the reverberating words Brandon had barked at him months before. *You run on flaming emotion, with little thought. You're heedless of how your actions will impact the future. Worse, you don't seem to care at all how they affect others. How can you be that entirely self-absorbed?*

A question that would possibly haunt him until the end of his days. Especially if he lost this young woman he'd taken for granted.

God, forgive me. And I beg You, work in her heart a miracle, that she could forgive me too.

Still tucked against his shoulder, Audrey drew in a shuddered breath. Then palms pressing against his shoulders, she nudged him away. He felt her withdrawal like the slow tearing of his heart, and the old ways of seeking his own will whatever the cost threatened to surge forth. Everything from pretty words and promises of all working out fine to well-practiced kisses that would coax her will to his, the tools he'd employed often enough to ensure his way dangled in his mind with tempting clarity. With unpracticed self-discipline, Brayden pushed them away as he let his arms drift to his sides.

Audrey fixed her attention on the blanket she twisted in her hands. "I just want to go home."

He couldn't have expected much different, but her response to his heartfelt apology and declaration of love drove like a javelin through his chest. He closed his empty hands and squeezed, absorbing the blow, and then nodded. "Okay."

Green eyes lifted to search his face, trepidation in them.

She didn't want him to go with her. Again, he had no right to expect otherwise. "If you can wait until after my classes today, I'll take you."

Her brow furrowed. Unclenching one hand, he lifted it to cradle her elbow. "I have to work this weekend, so I'll drive back tonight. You stay—" His voice cracked, and he had to swallow back hard emotion before he could continue. "Stay for however long you want."

The unspoken implication hung thick between them. Audrey looked back to her fidgeting hands and nodded. After a long silence in which it seemed they came unraveled further with every painful breath, she stopped rolling the thick yarn between her fingers and let her fingers fall still.

"You have class soon, right?"

Brayden's hand fell to his side. "Yes." He cleared his throat, forced himself to rise. "I should go." Slow to stand, he gathered his school bag. But the weight of all that hung in the balance stopped his departure, and he sought her face. "You'll wait for me to come back?"

Bottom lip caught beneath her teeth, she looked up to meet his desperate gaze. "You'll take me home?"

He nodded.

So did she. "I'll wait."

That was as far as she was willing to go. The most she could promise of the future. Beyond that, things did not look good.

—— *ele* ——

Audrey had tried to sleep during the two-hour drive that would deliver her where she'd told Brayden she wanted to go. Home.

It didn't feel like going home though. Fear clawed in her chest as the miles passed, delivering her ever closer to the place where this whole mess had begun. She longed for the familiar comfort of home, wanted nothing more than the reassuring strength of her mother's arms and the comfort of her dad's gentle hold. But there was the issue of truth that blocked that path.

She had yet to tell them all. This pit she'd dug herself into was so deep, she had no other choice but to confess and beg for grace. But that required her to face the people who had loved her, raised her, hoped for good things for her, and trusted her. Already, she had disappointed them. To tell them the full truth—that she'd been pregnant before she was married, had lied to them about why she got married the way she had, and hadn't told them about the grandchild they'd never know—it was overwhelming to think about.

Audrey wasn't sure she could do it.

As if sensing her burgeoning panic, Brayden broke the ninety-minute silence that had escorted them down the dark road. "I need to have an honest conversation with your dad."

She glanced at him, finding his jaw set in that determined look Brayden possessed. The one that made him look more like Brandon than ever. Stern and unmovable.

"You don't have to."

"Yes." Even in the dim light that filtered through the windshield offered by the full moon hanging over the hills, she could read resolve in his eyes. "Yes, I do."

"They're my parents," she argued. "It's my prob—"

"No, it's not your problem. Whatever you decide while you're at home, you need to know that I claim this. The damage done is my fault, and it's time I face your dad with it."

"They don't know about . . . about the baby."

"Also my doing." He reached across the small space between them and covered her hand. When he spoke again, it was with a softer tone. "I'll tell them."

Her heart twisted as she imagined her dad taking in that news. Tender man that Daddy was, he would feel the full stab of her betrayal, along with the harsh blow of losing a grandchild he hadn't even known about. It was nearly enough to summon the tears she'd thought had run dry.

"What . . . what will you tell him about us?" she whispered.

His thumb brushed over the inside of her wrist, and then his touch evaporated. "What do you want me to tell him?"

Audrey bit her lip. Even after a stretch of silence, she couldn't formulate an answer.

Brayden's fingertips feathered across her cheek. "I'll tell him you need a break. Some time to heal without the pressure of school. Is that okay?"

"Not—" Her words cut short. *Not that I don't think I can be with you.*

Again, his touch fell away, and he stared forward, focused on the stretch of road illuminated by the headlights. "I'll tell him as much or as little as you want about you and me right now. If you want me to tell him I broke your heart and you don't think you can trust me, I will."

His statement hung between them like a question he didn't really want to ask but was willing to leave in her hands.

This was not the Brayden she'd known. "Why?"

His grip on the steering wheel tightened. "My brother was really angry with me after we got married."

Seemed like a change in subject. Audrey wondered how he would piece the two together. "I know. I remember."

"He said some things that I should have listened to. Things that, even though I wanted to, I couldn't forget. He told me to be the man I wanted everyone to believe I was." He fell quiet while he guided the car into a turn.

"Seems like telling my dad everything will make him think the opposite."

"I'd rather he hears the truth of it from me than you." He glanced at her. "He should have heard the truth of it a long time ago. From me. It was the right thing to do, and I didn't do it."

The right thing to do . . . The phrase wove through her mind, stitching itself into her conscience.

The vehicle slowed, and Brayden turned off the highway and onto the road that would take her back home. One that could take her away from him, if she chose that path.

Her conscience rumpled uncomfortably, pressing that phrase in deeper. *The right thing to do . . .*

<hr/>

Sweat seeped from his pores as Brayden's heart hammered. Standing in the small room that doubled as Tim's office and Shay's craft room, located in the newly finished cottage his in-laws had moved into at some point since he'd married their daughter, Brayden pleaded with heaven for the will and strength to do what he'd promised Audrey. *Do the right thing.*

Tim might well kill him. What father wouldn't at least entertain homicidal thoughts against a man who had done what Brayden had done? He'd been a liar and a coward, right along with his selfishness. And to top it off, now he'd broken Audrey's heart.

All perfectly legitimate reasons for a father to strangle a son-in-law. As Brayden peered back over the previous months, he stood dumbfounded by his own idiocy all over again.

Tim strode into the room, and it seemed the air was vacuumed out. Did he truly have to share the whole story? He could stick to losing the baby—that was quite enough for all of them to deal with. Did he need to confess all his sins before this man? Tugging at his shirt as if it were suddenly a size XS constricting his large body, Brayden struggled to regain clear thought.

Come clean. You promised Audrey you would.

There was the sprout of resolve he needed. He reached for more, intentionally summoning Brandon's words that he'd previously hoped to bury. *Be the man you want everyone to believe you are.*

A good man. One who wears honor, even when it's uncomfortable. One who is honest and who admits his mistakes.

Mistakes? That seemed like an awfully benign word for all that he'd done.

"Thank you for bringing my daughter home." Tension wound Tim's voice tight. "It's been a long while."

Not a good start. Brayden rubbed the back of his neck. "I'm sorry for that."

Crossing his arms, Tim leaned against the door he'd pushed close. "There a reason for this sudden weekend visit?"

He was not making this easy, though that was as good a lead in as any. "Yes." Brayden cleared his throat as he jammed his hands into his pockets. "Audrey . . . needs a break."

"A break? From . . ."

From him. From their marriage. From life. "The thing is, sir." Brayden forced himself to look the man in the eye. "The thing is, we were expecting."

"Expecting?"

"A . . . a baby."

Tim's brows lifted. "When?"

"January first."

Those brows flew clear up to his hairline. "That's less than two months from now."

Heat flooded Brayden's whole body, and he had to stiffen his jaw against the surge of grief that welled up. "Yes. But no."

"No?"

"The baby died. A little over a month ago. Audrey delivered our son at the end of September. He was stillborn."

Tim's entire expression collapsed into shocked pain. "Your . . . son?" As he processed, his mouth tightened, and he swallowed visibly several times. "Why . . . how could you not tell us?"

This was the juncture, the point where Brayden could turn down the coward's path, as he'd done before. Or.

Or he could be the man he wanted people to think he was. A better man. The man Audrey had hoped she'd married. He breathed in, hoping there was some untapped courage to be found buried deep inside himself.

"Audrey wanted to tell you. I asked her to put it off. It's my fault."

"Why would you do that?"

"Because I didn't want you to know."

Tim stared unflinching at him, his silence demanding Brayden finish the entirety of his confession.

"I didn't want you to know that she was pregnant before we were married."

A hard mask of anger glared back at him. "It was a cover-up."

Scalding shame poured over him. "Yes."

"That was why you married her."

God, do I have to admit that? Brayden squeezed his eyes shut. "Yes." The word, a harsh whisper, barely made it off his tongue.

Suddenly strong fists were at his shoulders, bunching his shirt. Before Brayden had his vision refocused, he was spun around and his back slammed against the door. "You took what wasn't yours, got my daughter pregnant, and then stole her from my home?" Tim's voice was fury, but not a shout. It was a river of outrage and undammed pain. "She was innocent! She was only ever a good girl. How could you do such a thing?"

Tim's righteous anger poured down on Brayden's raw heart, mingling with the self-incrimination that had already pooled there. He slumped against the door, not willing to fight against the bear who had him pinned. "I know." His voice cracked. "I know she was. I don't know why I did what I did. But it was me, Tim. It was all me."

The fierce grip that held him against the door eased, and Tim's fury melted into heartbroken disappointment.

Brayden gripped the man's arms and held fast, as if Tim would collapse under the burden of emotion. "It was me," he repeated. "Hate me, not her. She only followed my lead, and I did everything I could to make sure that she did."

Posture slumped, Tim backed away. Brayden held on to his arms until he stepped out of reach. "The baby—a boy?"

Vision swimming, Brayden nodded.

"It wasn't because . . . she didn't try to—"

He shook his head. "There was something not right with his heart. Audrey did nothing wrong."

Tim exhaled a shaking breath and reached behind him to grip the edge of his small desk. In a space of tense silence, he gazed at the floor near Brayden's feet.

"Audrey is heartbroken," Brayden whispered.

"She never said a word."

Pressing his lips, Brayden could only nod. "I'm sorry."

Another gulf of silence widened between them. Tim rubbed his fore-head and sniffed. Finally he looked back at Brayden. "She's here to recover?"

"Yes." Unease unfurled in his chest. "She's . . . she's had a hard time."

"Because of the baby." The statement held a strong hint of suspicion, laced with accusation. There was more to it, and Tim wasn't going to be blindsided again.

What was right was sometimes a blurry thing. Brayden braced in the pause between them, quietly asking for heaven's light to break open so that he would know the right thing to do. Finally, shoulders sagging, Brayden once again met his father-in-law's eyes. "Our marriage was built on lies. On my drive to hide what I didn't want known. That's not a very secure start."

"No." One eyebrow tipped up, and Tim crossed his arms. "It isn't."

"You can imagine, then, that things between Audrey and me aren't great."

A hard stare was Tim's only response.

"I know that's my fault. I'm not dumping her here and running."

"What are you doing?"

"She wanted to come home. And"—Brayden rubbed his jaw—"she doesn't want me to stay with her right now. Since I'm the one who got us into this mess, I guess I figured I owed her at least that. I have to work, so I'll head back tonight."

Disapproval pulsed in the small room, and Brayden peeked at the man who glared at him.

"I don't know what else to do. Losing our son was devastating and—" And he'd broken her heart further by keeping secrets from her. But Audrey hadn't given him permission to share that part. Brayden couldn't deny that he'd been relieved by that fact. "I want her to be okay. Honestly, I do."

Tim's stern, angry expression softened, and after a moment, he sighed. Then nodded. "I know that pain, Brayden."

Which pain?

"Shay and I lost four. Audrey was the only child we could carry full term. After she was born, we didn't have the heart to try for more." Tim stepped forward and, startling Brayden, laid a compassionate hand on his shoulder. "It hurts. It hurts deeply, son. I'm sorry."

Brayden couldn't stop the quivering of his chin, nor could he stem the rush of hot tears that glazed his eyes. It wasn't only the shared pain of loss, but this undeserved grace offered. Brayden had been a thief in Tim's home, taking a treasure most dear to the man. Tim had no obligation to offer compassion.

"Have you named him?" Tim's question came on a choked voice.

Brayden could only shake his head. They should have by now. They should have the day his small body had been placed in Brayden's palms. But they hadn't. It was almost like giving the baby a name would be an end to it. Shouldn't they want that closure?

Tim offered no rebuke. Only an understanding nod. Could one understand something that didn't make sense?

"Will you be back?" he asked instead.

Sorrow looped around Brayden's heart. "When Audrey is ready." Such a vague answer couldn't sit well with Tim. It certainly didn't with Brayden. But he'd promised her space and that he wouldn't push, wouldn't manipulate. If that meant he'd be exposed for the failure he was, then . . .

Well then, he'd be exposed. God already knew it all, anyway.

For a long moment, Tim studied Brayden. Then, wearing a weary expression, he nodded and moved for the door. Before turning the knob, though, he paused and glanced back to Brayden.

"Do you love her?"

For a father, that was the heart of everything, wasn't it? Brayden felt the weight of responsibility alongside the pressing of what he truly did feel for his wife—for this man's daughter. He wished back so much of what had been between he and Audrey. Wished he'd been the Murphy she'd believed him to be. But she was his wife, and he couldn't wish that away.

Even if he'd do it all differently if he could, he had no desire to change the fact that they were married.

Brayden lifted his gaze and lined it up square with Tim's. "I do."

—⁓—

She slept on and off for two days.

Audrey hadn't realized how purely exhausted she'd been. It seemed strange that she would be so, as she hadn't done much of anything in over a month. But this sleep, in her parents' home, it had been actually restful, though she had to admit, the bed felt lonely.

How was Brayden doing? He texted her a handful of times every day. Nothing demanding or intrusive. Just, *I made it back. Good night. Good morning. I hope your day goes well. I'm thinking of you.* And last night . . . *I love you Audrey.*

Sitting alone at the table, her bowl of apple cinnamon oatmeal cooling, Audrey's heart squeezed with warm ache as she reread that text.

"Good morning." Mom's soft voice reached her from the back door, which was behind Audrey.

Audrey glanced over her shoulder, barely able to meet Mom's gaze. The past two days had been mostly quiet between her and her parents. Brayden had told her dad the truth about them—about why they'd married, and their sad news. She'd overheard her father's anger as she'd hidden in her room, and it had rattled her deeply. Daddy wasn't the yelling sort of man. Calm and gentle, Daddy was ever in control of his emotions.

And Mom? Mom seemed unsteady, which was certainly not normal. Mom was the confident, get-stuff-done sort of woman. The kind who addressed things head on. But not this. She'd given Audrey a wide berth and had seemed uncertain when they were together.

Everything in Audrey's world was topsy-turvy. She just wanted to find firm footing. Maybe then she'd know what to do.

Mom approached on slow, soft strides, both hands gripping capped paper cups. As she lowered onto a chair beside Audrey, the sweet aroma of crisp fall apples and warm cinnamon gentled the uncertain silence between them. Audrey inhaled, her eyes slipping closed.

In that smell, there was years of cherished memories. Multiple trips to the orchard, apple picking, hours spent together in the Alexanders' big kitchen, where she and Megan helped Mom peel and core apples or wash and slice them to pile them in the steam juicer. The girls would make themselves nearly sick eating fresh, crisp apple slices and the crunchy ribbons of peels. And their reward? Freshly baked apple turnovers and this. Homebrewed cider, the taste of which Audrey hadn't found a match.

Suddenly grief washed over Audrey like a tidal wave. Shoulders shaking, she began to sob. And there was Mom, work-strong arms gripping her shoulders, taking her in.

"Oh, Audrey." She sighed, a touch of tears in her voice.

"Mom, I've ruined everything that was beautiful and good."

As if she were a five-year-old girl with a broken toy, not a nine-teen-year-old woman with a splintered life, Mom tugged her off the chair and onto her lap. There she sat, cradled in the arms of a woman whose heart had to have been broken these past many months by Audrey's choices. It only made the grief heavier.

"All is not ruined, love," Mom whispered.

"It feels like it."

"I know. But that is sorrow and regret, Audrey. They will not remain forever."

"How do you know?"

"The Bible says it. Weeping lasts for the night, but joy comes in the morning."

"There have been so many nights of weeping, Mom. And no joy."

A gentle teary laugh moved through Mom's embrace. "It will come, sweetheart."

Audrey tucked her head against her mother's shoulder, and Mom's arms tightened around her. When the surge of tears subsided, she brushed them from her face. "Mom? What should I do?"

"You're talking about you and Brayden?"

Still snuggled against her, Audrey nodded.

A long space of quiet drifted between them, and then Mom sighed. "I don't know what to say."

Audrey sat up and looked at the woman who had held her. Mom always knew what to say. She had always given good advice. "Mom?"

With a gentle nudge, she urged Audrey back to her own chair and then sipped her cider. "I know what I probably should say. That is that marriage is sacred to God." Her mouth tightened, and roiling emotion made her expression almost harsh. "But I have to confess that right now I'm so mad at Brayden that I can't bring myself to say it."

Such an unexpected response split Audrey's heart. She found in that wedging a place that rose fierce to defend her husband. "He forced nothing on me, Mom. I chose this."

Mom studied her. Searching for a lie in that? Or perhaps there was a touch of wonder in that searching gaze. "He told your dad that he loves you."

Audrey could only nod as she traced the ridge of the mug containing her cider.

"Had he been good to you?"

"He's taken care of me."

"That isn't what I asked."

"He has not ever been unkind. Selfish, sometimes, but not unkind. And he works hard to make sure we are both taken care of."

"That doesn't sound exactly like love to me."

Audrey bit her lip and searched for the strength to tell the truth. "He didn't love me at first. He was still angry about his previous girlfriend when he and I met. They'd been together for years, and Brayden had planned to marry her. She broke up with him to marry someone else."

Anger darkened Mom's steady look. "He used you, then."

"I knew all this. Brandon and Megan had told me—they both warned me that Brayden wasn't in a good place. I . . . I ignored them."

The flash of outrage dimmed.

"I guess I thought maybe I'd rescue him, or something stupid like that. That when he finally got over Leah, I would be right there."

"And he'd love you for it?"

Clasping her hands, Audrey nodded. "I think I realized how dumb that was last spring. But by then . . ."

"Then you found out you were pregnant?"

Heat flooded her face. "Yes."

"And he proposed because of the baby?"

"Yes."

"But he didn't love you."

Audrey shook her head.

"Oh, honey. I wish we had known."

"I know, Mom." Audrey made herself look at her mom. "I'm sorry I lied to you."

Mom nodded, swallowing.

"What would you have told me to do, if you had known the truth then?"

"I don't know for certain." Mom shook her head and let her gaze drift out the window. The gray clouds hanging low over the evergreen trees had the look and smell of snow about them. "I'm not sure it matters. Who knows if what I would have said would have been right. We only see what's in front of us, you know? But I know this for sure, Audrey. Your dad and I wouldn't have rejected you. Our love for you is not so fragile that it could be severed with disappointment."

Quiet fell. Audrey sipped on the cooled cider, wondering what advice Mom would give now, after she'd heard the full run of it.

Well, most of it.

She couldn't bring herself to share about seeing Brayden and Leah together at the union. Not simply because that wound was too fresh, too much. Actually, the jab of it had scabbed over surprisingly fast. Realizing it was so for the first time, Audrey checked that cut specifically, wondering why it seemed to heal more quickly than it should.

I swear. There's nothing going on between Leah and me.

I love you, Audrey.

Sometime between that dark day and this less dreary one, Audrey had come to believe her husband. Did that make her a fool?

More, she didn't want to share that part with her mom because she wanted to protect Brayden. He'd already exposed himself to her father and had gained the rarity of Dad's outrage. He didn't need to be made yet smaller in her parents' eyes. Not when he'd claimed all responsibility, not when he'd tried as best as he could to make things easier for her with them. If they were to make it through this low point of their young marriage, she wanted Brayden to have a shot at gaining her parents' esteem.

Were they going to make it?

"What changed?" Mom asked, derailing Audrey's internal exam.

"Changed?"

"Brayden told your dad that he loves you. Quite sincerely."

The very question Audrey should have asked her husband but hadn't. "I don't know." Her mind went back to being muddled, her heart lost and afraid.

"I'm so sorry, Audrey. I know right now your heart simply hurts, and I'm so very sorry for it." Mom reached across the space to take her hand. "Keep being honest. And pray for direction. You'll know the right thing to do."

Later that night, after an afternoon spent beside the river, bundled up against November's chill and an ongoing conversation with God, Mom's tender compassion and gentle confidence in her settled warmly on Audrey's heart. And with it, a few passing lines she'd uttered earlier in the conversation.

Marriage is sacred to God.

In the kindest way possible, Mom had told her exactly what she needed to hear.

And by their living example, her parents had shown her what she needed to know. *Our love for you is not so fragile that it could be severed with disappointment.*

The right thing was in front of her, difficult though it might be.

Chapter Twenty-One

(IN WHICH THERE ARE FRIENDS AND THERE ARE BROTHERS)

"Brayden." The low timbre of the voice on the other end of the call was familiar. He owned the Murphy tone. But this brother didn't often call. "It's Jacob. Brandon told me a little bit of what's going on. I'm just calling in case you need someone to talk to."

A flash of resentment flared against Brandon's interference. Typical. Brandon had been forever sending someone to him to fix this or address that. Drunk at a bar? Send Jackson, the one who'd been drunk when he got married. Surely they'd have a heart-to-heart and Brayden could be reset on the right path. Trouble with his girlfriend? Brandon had contacted Matt in an attempt to have Brayden see that maybe he was holding on to something that wasn't God's best for him. Bomb a test? Talk to Tyler, advised Brandon. He could surely motivate you to overcome adversity. After all, the man had lost his leg.

Tossing his backpack into his car, Brayden suppressed a growl and followed his pack into the vehicle. Brandon meant well. If nothing else proved that, there was his brother's rock-solid support of Brayden over the past couple of months.

"Hey, Jacob." He cleared his throat, just in case a hint of irritation lingered in his voice. "Thanks for the call. I'm not sure I can talk about it though."

He and Jacob weren't close. Truthfully, Jacob had never been super close to any of the brothers. To Connor, maybe, but Connor was a little bit like Brandon. The do-the-right-thing kind of guy who gave that advice consistently, whether it was asked for or not. Connor was also the guy who faithfully kept tabs on everyone because he felt like he should. Again, the do-the-right-thing guy. But Brayden wasn't talking to Connor. It'd been Jacob who called.

Which was, on second thought, interesting. Jacob was Connor's and Brandon's opposite. In fact, of all of Brayden's brothers, Jacob and he were probably the most alike in personality. Meaning they lived their own lives and tended to withdraw from the rest of them while doing so.

"I get it, brother." Jacob's gentle tone struck Brayden as . . . different. Jacob was a bit of a poker man. He didn't reveal his hand, so to speak. Ever. Any trace of emotion from that brother was like spotting a unicorn. Didn't happen. But there it was. "Listen, Bray. I don't know how much of my story you know, but I'm just calling to say that I get it. Kate and I had several miscarriages."

Brayden didn't know what to say to that. He didn't want to talk about it, actually. Even so, his mouth opened. "Thanks for the empathy, Jacob. But the truth is, losing our son is only some of it. Audrey's back with her parents. I don't know if we're going to make it."

Whoa. For a guy who didn't want to talk about it, he'd just spilled his guts.

"Man, Bray." The compassion in Jacob's words were deeper than Brayden could have imagined. "Brother, I have *been* there."

Brayden leaned forward, intending to start his car, thinking that with his last confession, this conversation would be short lived. What guy really wanted to discuss another's failing marriage? No one he knew. But at Jacob's response, Brayden froze, then withdrew his fingers from his keys as he leaned back. "What?"

"Kate nearly left me."

The statement hit Brayden like an iron wall. From everything Brayden had ever seen, Kate adored Jacob. Almost to the point of being ridiculous. "When?"

"When she bought the skoolie. Gert was her way out of our marriage."

"I thought you guys bought that thing for her writing. So she could start her blog."

"No." A small, sad chuckle broke Jacob's speech. "Gert was Kate's purchase, and she definitely did not intend for me to go with her on the road. The truth is, I chased after a life that looked good on the surface, but what Kate and I had was a home full of debt and a marriage that was nearly entirely empty."

How had Brayden not known this? He'd been in high school when Jacob and Kate had become boondockers. Could he have truly been so wrapped up in his own small world that he'd been blind to what was going on with his own brother?

Clearly, yes, that had been exactly the case. What else had he not known?

"Look, Brayden, I don't know your story, but I can tell from what Brandon has told me, and from the little bit I hear from you now, that you're in a hard spot. I promise you, based on my own life, God isn't afraid of your hard places. Your messes don't scare Him. My marriage is a miracle, and what Kate and I have now is real. It's pure. But it didn't come easy, and it didn't happen without us going through some really hard things. So if that's where you're at now, in the hard places, just don't give up too easily. Wounds heal. Repentance and forgiveness are powerful. And love—pure, selfless love—it overcomes."

Between being dumbfound and tossed back into the waves of raw emotion, Brayden couldn't summon words.

"I'll be praying for you and Audrey, little brother."

He had to swallow twice before he could say anything. Even then, "Thanks" was the only cracked word he could manage.

Jacob hung up, leaving Brayden to contemplate all that he'd said. It shocked him anew to realize how much of his brother's life he'd been unaware of. To hear that Jacob had walked through such a valley . . .

Had Brayden truly thought his brothers' lives had been all ease? That they'd had these perfect stories that cost them nothing, that had worked without effort? That they had just *happened*?

No one's life was like that. Everyone walked through hard things. All made mistakes—sometimes massive ones. How ridiculously ignorant it had been of him to imagine the things he'd envied his brothers for were the entirety of their lives, their stories. That wasn't life. And believing otherwise had proven to be a disaster.

So what was he going to do with *his* life?

Brayden paused on that thought. Let the question linger until it sprouted wings and took flight, changing into a prayer. A single word returned to him in response.

Surrender.

———

"How are you by now, my friend?" Megan looped an arm through Audrey's as they wandered down the dirt lane that connected the Smith cottage and the riverside guest house—which should now be referenced as Brandon and Megan's house, as they'd spent a year living happily married there. *Brandon and Megan's house.* Audrey repeated the new label in her mind, and a splinter of envy threatened to crack as she did so.

Megan loved her husband. Brandon adored his wife. As different as the two were—like the softness of cotton to the firmness of steel—they were a stunning complement to each other. They made each other better. Brandon firmed up the places in Megan that were wishy-washy and a tad silly. Megan softened Brandon. And now, a little more than a year past their wedding, Audrey could see at a glance they loved. They loved deeply, beautifully.

In a way that Audrey had once believed possible for Brayden and herself.

Is your love so fragile?

The clouds of yesterday had cleared, leaving behind a diamond frosting of snow glittering across the river valley. Evergreens looked silvery in the sunshine, gleaming with sparkling white. The river, not seen from the road, rushed with predictable steadiness, filling the spaces of silence between friends with a comfortable reminder that some things remained throughout the seasons. Audrey took in the beauty of the moment and contrasted it with the steadiness of that river.

Would she be more like the dusting of snow, sure to melt within the hour, or the river beyond her view?

Within her chest, she sensed a rooting. A new growth where there had only been barren soil. "I am better, I think," she said, finally responding to Megan's question.

Megan drew her in close to her side. "I'm glad. You seem more rested."

There was that. And there was a little perspective. Also, there was Brayden's persistent though gentle texts. A few of which were startlingly new from a man she thought she'd discovered all about. Like last night he'd written, *I am praying, Audrey. More now than I ever have. As I should have done from the beginning of us. I pray for you, that the brokenness of your heart will mend. And for me, that I would learn how to be the man I wish I was. And for us.*

I know you are still deciding, and I give you all the time you need. But I feel like maybe you need to know where my heart is on that. Just so it's clear, I still want us. I want us better than before.

How could reading that not move her heart? Brayden had always wielded the power of persuasion. But that had been entirely *other*. She'd wished he was there with her last night. That she could hear the warm depth of his voice and see the beautiful richness of his eyes.

"Megan?" Audrey leaned into the friend at her side. "Have you and Brandon ever had a serious fight?"

Megan laughed so loud, the sound bounced through the trees. "Do you remember how we were at the beginning? I think he hoped I'd fall into the river and be carried away, and I might have fantasized about a tree rolling down the hill and taking him out."

Audrey chuckled. Indeed, she did remember the pair of them when Brandon first arrived as Megan's arranged fiancé. A worse idea, it seemed, had never been conceived. "But that's not what I mean. Since you've been married. Have you had a blowout after you fell in love?"

Snorting, Megan shook Audrey's arm. "You mean like when I demanded he trade in that hideous truck he owns for something respectable, and he told me I was going to have to shoot him and pry the keys from his dead fingers before I could get rid of it?"

"You fought about his dumb truck?"

"Like it was a matter of life and death." Megan slipped a sly smirk toward Audrey. "And for the record, *he* slept in the guest room that night. No way I was giving up my bed. Also, just between you and me, I *will* get rid of that hideous beast before I die."

Shaking her head, Audrey rolled her eyes. "Something like that though, it doesn't really matter."

"Oh, we were mad enough, you would have thought the fate of eternity rested with that issue." Megan slipped an arm around Audrey as they continued down the road. "The thing is, Audrey, people fight. Married people fight. Over things that matter and things that are dumb. That's just life."

"I know. I guess."

"What's this really about?"

"I just keep wondering if Brayden and I have a future."

Diverting toward a large boulder, Megan stopped and turned to face Audrey. "Do you want a future with him?"

"Yes." That answer came surprisingly easy. Then again, it shouldn't have been surprising. The reason she'd done all this had been because she wanted Brayden. But she'd wanted the version she'd imagined him to be back then. A little more like Brandon, perhaps. Reliable and steady—just with a hearty dash of more fun than Brandon exhibited.

That hadn't been fair of her, to assume that because Brayden looked like his brother, he would act like his brother. And anyway, so much of what had hooked in Audrey's heart after she'd spent time with Brayden was who he was. Determined as anything but laid back too. He'd loved to tease and laugh, but he worked every bit as hard as anyone when times called for it. And he *saw* Audrey. She hadn't been a backdrop for the Alexanders. For Megan. That had never shifted with him.

Except when she'd seen him with Leah.

Was that why she'd so easily believed the implications of Victoria's misinformed impression? There it was, the heart of the matter. She'd feared from the first day that she'd fade into the background of Brayden's life. She didn't want to be any woman's understudy in her own story. That had been the conflict with Megan over a year before. And now she was allowing that insecurity to jeopardize her marriage.

"Audrey?"

Snapping her attention back to Megan, Audrey suddenly realized she'd been staring at the peaks in the distance, not listening when Megan had clearly been talking. "I'm sorry, what?"

"I asked, what are you going to do about it?"

Audrey blew out a slow, fortifying breath, the puff of it a drift of white before her. "I guess we should talk."

Megan settled a smile that was all tender pride. "You were always the smarter one of the two of us."

"What does that mean?"

With a shrug, she turned to continue their walk on the road. "I'd have told him that he married me and he wasn't getting out of it, so he'd better figure out how to make me happy or risk misery for the rest of his life."

At that Audrey snorted, and Megan laughed. They both knew it wasn't true in the least. But Audrey appreciated the reason to smile. It made the light cracking through her darkness brighter.

◦ℓℓ◦

Brayden walked beside his wife with all the jittery nerves of a twelve-year-old boy working up the gumption to confess to his crush that he liked her.

Oh, but this was so much weightier than that. He couldn't shrug away the sense that *everything* was converging on this moment. After answering Audrey's call earlier that day, he'd felt as though his heart was scattered in a million different directions, and he had no idea if it'd ever be whole again.

All, it seemed, lay in this woman's hands.

"*I think we need to talk.*" She had said on that call. "*Face to face.*"

A good thing, or no?

When he'd arrived, parking in front of the Smiths' cottage, she'd met him at the front door. For a brief moment, their eyes connected, and he thought he saw softness within those green depths. But then she'd looked away, snatching her coat that must have hung near the door.

"Will you walk with me?" she'd asked.

In the minutes since, she'd not said anything. Tension unfurled like emerging weeds, and Brayden focused on opening and closing his fists to keep himself from giving in to the urge to take her by the shoulders and demand that she love him back.

They wove through the maze of trees, Brayden following her lead all the while wishing she'd stop and say what she wanted him to hear. Unless, of course, she wanted to say things he didn't want to hear.

Finally, they came to the bank of the river, it's edges glossy with a thin layer of clear ice. A cold north wind stirred the treetops, sending flakes of snow off the boughs to flutter like glitter in the crisp air. If he wasn't so bound up with anxiety, he might even think this moment romantic.

Audrey paused, hugging herself as she breathed white against the late-afternoon chill. As if approaching a skittish animal, Brayden slowly closed the gap between them until his feet stopped parallel to hers.

"I was thinking Caleb." Her whisper cracked on the name.

Brayden sucked in a breath as everything inside constricted. He knew what she meant. "Caleb."

She nodded, still not looking at him. "Caleb Murphy."

He reached for her hand, and she didn't deny him the connection. Though his throat was tight and raw, he forced words from his lips. "I like that." Caleb Murphy. He would have it etched on the plaster footprints the hospital had given them. As he thought on that, a gentle peace closed over the ache of losing his son. Shutting his eyes, his thoughts turned toward heaven. *Jesus, will You tell Caleb I love him?*

The hand in his squeezed gently, and he heard the shuddering release of Audrey's breath. With it, he sensed some of her grief ease.

"Tell me what happened." Her voice came soft, and then she shifted her feet until she faced him. She blinked against the sheen in her eyes.

"You mean with Leah?"

She nodded. "The truth."

Searching that gaze, he found no sharp accusation in it. Her watch was open, and it summoned yearning from his heart.

He dipped a single nod, glad to have a chance to say what he should have told her months before. "Leah showed up on campus at the beginning of the semester. I saw her the second week of school, and she saw me. She wanted to catch up, so we went to the union, and she bought me a shake. There, she told me that her husband is deployed for six months, and she transferred to be where she would know someone." Heat pushed away the chill that had settled on his cheeks. "I was uncomfortable that she was there, and I should have told you. That day that you thought there was something wrong, and I got upset at you for asking me about it?"

Audrey nodded.

"That was what was wrong."

"Why didn't you just tell me?"

"I don't know, Audrey. Honestly, I don't. I just didn't want the situation at all. It was like all the anger I'd thought I was done with from before resurged. I was mad at Leah for transferring there, and I was mad at her for thinking that I'd be her best buddy. For insisting that somehow there'd still be a place for her with me. I was mad that I couldn't just have an easy, comfortable life without complicated things getting in the way."

She flinched. "Things . . . like me?"

"No." Brayden reached for her, shaking his head. "Audrey, I didn't love you in the beginning like I should have. I admit that, and I wish I'd been different then. But I never thought of you as being in the way. Not ever. One of the reasons I wanted to get married the way we did was so that I wouldn't worry about you all the time. You would be right there with me."

Her gaze, held fast on him, softened more. Brayden took that in and used it as fuel for more courage. "What else do you need me to tell you?"

"Do you love her?" Her response sounded choked. "Is that why you didn't want to tell me?"

He shook his head while his fingers tightened on her arm. "There was a time when I thought I loved Leah. I don't even know if that was true though. I just wanted the life I had planned."

"Now all your plans have been undone."

"Revised." Brayden dared to lean nearer. "*I* am being revised. I can't say that's a bad thing, even if it doesn't feel very good."

His forehead touched hers, and she tipped her face up willingly. "Whatever it was I felt for Leah is over. I was disappointed by her, and ugly for it. But I'm seeing now that sometimes disappointment is a gift. But this, between you and me? Being without you this week has been far beyond disappointment. I want us. With all my heart, I want us."

The weight and warmth of her hands sank through the fabric of his jacket, and his heart responded with a hopeful jolt.

"Audrey?" Her name felt almost like prayer from his lips, whispered with reverence and daring hope beyond all reason.

"Okay, Bray." Her lids slipped over those emerald gems as the warmth of her breath tempted his mouth.

"Okay?"

The slightest move of her head sufficed as a nod. "Let's go home."

It wasn't a promise. But it was hope, and more than he deserved. Unable to withstand the temptation of her lips, he brushed them softly with his own. Just once.

"Okay." And then he took her hand. Later, he drove her home.

Chapter Twenty-Two

(IN WHICH BRAYDEN FINALLY KNOWS WHAT HE REALLY WANTS)

Brayden sat in the circle of his brothers, the six of them gathered around a mound of firewood waiting to be loaded and then stacked. The Thanksgiving weekend spent all together at the lodge where Matt and Lauren had fallen in love, and where now Connor and Sadie lived and worked full time, had been a relaxing time. Up until that morning. Saturday brunch was Mom's favorite meal of all time, so it came as no surprise that before they were scattered back to their homes, the Murphys would spend one more boisterous meal, this time in the large front gathering space of the lodge. It was there that they discovered why Connor had asked them all to come.

Sadie was sick. Her cancer had returned, and the prognosis was heartbreaking. Connor had barely made it through the telling.

"We didn't want to ruin the holidays." Connor had closed his announcement quietly. "But we didn't think it was right not to tell you."

Not a single Murphy had a dry eye. This was devastating. Truly and utterly devastating.

Now, as the brothers stood round the mound of work to be done, a collective held breath stole over them. It was Matt who finally cracked the heavy silence. Hand on Connor's shoulder, Matt spoke with reverence. "Can I pray for you, brother?"

Connor's mask of composure, which he'd managed to reassemble after brunch was cleared and the Murphy boys had applied boots and gloves to help him resupply the lodge's wood stock, wavered. "Every single day, if you don't mind."

"That's a promise," Matt said.

"Here too." Jackson moved forward, gripping Connor's other shoulder.

"Same." The commitments echoed from every brother, including Brayden.

"Let's lift our brother up together right now, boys." Matt met each man's eyes as he spoke, and then he bowed. "Father God . . ."

Matt didn't make it past that before the tears began to seep from Brayden's eyes. *Why so many valleys, Lord? Why this? Why Connor and Sadie?*

The group prayer wasn't long, though Tyler and Brandon both put voice to their heart cries. Then the circle of brothers broke loose, each man gathering the split wood Connor must have worked on for several weeks and loading it into the back of a truck. Once the truck bed was full, five of the seven brothers piled into the cab and headed back toward the lodge.

Brayden stayed behind with Connor.

Sweat had seeped through Brayden's hair and sat against his stocking cap. He tugged it from his head as he fell into step beside Connor.

"I hear you've had your own season of darkness, Brayden." Connor shoved his hands into his coat pockets as he wandered down the road.

Brayden couldn't fathom how Connor would want to talk about that, given his own painful circumstances. He nodded anyway. Then, surprising himself, he said, "I don't understand God."

Slow steps coming to a halt, Connor looked at Brayden. "Sometimes I don't either."

"This doesn't make sense." Brayden gestured toward Connor. "A lot of my struggles have been my own doing. I get that, though I wish I hadn't dragged Audrey into the pit with me. But this? I can't make sense of Sadie being sick again. Doesn't God know Reid needs his mom? Doesn't He know you love your wife? And my son—" His rush of words cut short.

Connor nodded, pain etched in every line of his face. "Trust me, I ask these questions too. There has been plenty of yelling at God from this Murphy."

"How . . ." Brayden paused, took in the steadiness of his older brother. Brokenhearted, yes. But steady even so.

Shaking his head, as if he knew the question Brayden couldn't quite form, Connor slipped a hand from his pocket and gripped Brayden's arm. "Hold on to Jesus. That's all I know to do, Bray."

"But you love her, and you chose to marry her and be Reid's dad when you didn't have to. It seems like that should count for something."

"It counts." Connor laid his palm over his chest. "It counts for everything. I'd do it all again, even knowing how this feels right now. I'd gladly do it again. Love is worth it." He stepped closer and replaced his hand on Brayden's shoulder. "Love your wife, little brother. Love her like you might not get tomorrow. Because you might not."

Brayden nodded, a tear slipping down his cheek and settling on the edge of his trimmed beard. "But what about the ache?"

Blowing out a slow, steady breath, Connor lifted his gaze and set it toward the lodge. Brayden had little doubt that what moved in his brother's chest was painful beyond words, but though Connor winced, there was also something else. A mysterious yielding when it seemed the man should be thrashing. Something so *other* that it seemed divine.

"Let it press us into Jesus," Connor said, but it seemed he was no longer talking to Brayden. With a small tip of his chin upward, he shut his eyes and held for a moment.

Brayden had the sense that he was witnessing a holy moment of surrender.

Later, after all the Murphys had gathered for one last time that weekend and Dad had uttered a broken prayer over his family, Brayden held Audrey's hand as they climbed the stairs and quietly made their way to their room.

Love your wife, little brother.

As he sat alone on the bed, Audrey having slipped through the slider door and now standing on the balcony overlooking the lake, Brayden clenched his fists.

He wanted to. God help him, he wanted to be more like Connor. More like Matt and Jacob, Jackson, and Tyler. More like Brandon. And finally, after years of envying the brothers God had blessed him with, Brayden realized that it wasn't their lives, and the blessings he thought he should automatically have, that he needed. That he longed for. He wanted the relationship each had with God.

It was like at long last, his vision cleared, and he understood what he had confused before. His brothers had learned to walk with God. To hold on to Jesus. And that made them the men they were. Flawed, yes. Men whose stories weren't perfect and whose lives weren't always easy. But men who loved Jesus and who let Jesus love through them.

Let that be me too. As Brayden sent that silent, surrendered prayer upward, his clenched fingers unfurled.

And then he sought the woman he'd married.

Steam drifted upward from the navy glass of the lake below, creating an eerie beauty. The white light of the full moon reflected off the distant deeper waters. The view from the lodge was stunning. But it didn't capture Audrey's attention quite the way it had the evening before.

This night, as she stood on the balcony outside of the room she and Brayden had been gifted, her gaze had been caught by the couple who had walked hand in hand down the pathway toward the water, and now that same couple stood arm in arm on the end of the dock. Everything had shifted with the news shared earlier that day, and now Audrey could only see them.

Her heart twisted.

They loved. By all accounts from the Murphy family members, Connor and Sadie loved deeply.

How could this be fair? To be gifted with such abiding tenderness that they would make it through one hard battle with cancer already, now only to face it again?

"It's . . . it doesn't look good."

Connor's broken admission to the family replayed in her mind. Later, in the privacy of their room, she'd asked Brayden, with his growing medical knowledge, what that meant exactly. She hadn't wanted to investigate it herself.

Brayden had rubbed the back of his neck, looked to the floor, and then shook his head. "The outlook for recurrent cervical cancer isn't good." He sounded like he was reciting from a textbook, but he looked devastated.

Audrey had stepped toward him, reached for his hand, and held it. As she reflected on that, it occurred to her that it'd been one of the few times in the week since they'd stood together by the river and named their son that she'd made a physical move toward him. Brayden had squeezed her fingers gently and then simply stood there unmoving until she'd stepped away.

She should have given him more, she realized now. Offered more comfort. Why couldn't she get past this wall in her heart? She'd thought going back home with him would do it. They'd get past this steep hill between them. But it hadn't been so.

Not until you forgive.

The thought provoked pressure in her chest. Forgive him, she would do . . . just as soon as she was certain he wouldn't break her heart again.

Was that how it worked?

A leery discomfort moved within her as she sensed the real answer to that question. Rather than let it form into words that she could no longer push away, Audrey focused on the splendor of nature that opened wide before her. The edges of the bay were lined with white, the snow brushing the rocks of the beach, gathering the light from the moon. On either side of the water, evergreen trees rode the gentle slopes upward, their shadowed boughs frosted with a dusting of snow and glittering softly against the darkness. Straight ahead, the mouth of the bay opened wide to the depths and breadth of the vast lake, the glow of the moon rippling on the waters. The evening, though cold, was still and lovely.

And the couple on the dock continued to beckon her attention. Surely in their six years of marriage, there had been troubles. Long nights of arguments. Wounds carelessly inflicted. Trusts broken. Things that needed forgiven. Hadn't there been?

Was her plight truly so unique in this world? People messed up. They did things that were selfish. Manipulated. Wounded those they cared about. Brayden wasn't exclusive in that. Truth was, Audrey had done those things too.

The silhouettes on the dock moved, Sadie turning into Connor. Connor wrapped his wife up close and laid his head on hers.

Longing stirred something that felt like life in her chest. She watched, mesmerized, a distant intruder on this sacred moment between a man and his wife, unable to turn away and unable to brush off the realization that she was witnessing the miracle of love. The beauty of it. But only from a distance, only the surface of it.

She wanted that, what she saw in that image, that moment. But only that. Only the surface beauty of it.

That was foolish. Complete blindness. Because what Connor and Sadie shared clearly had depth, and that couldn't have come easy.

What Matt and Lauren shared had depth. A depth that implied work.

She knew from the well-known story of Tyler and Rebecca that what they had together only came because of stubborn love and determined forgiveness.

And more recently, she'd found out from Brayden that Jacob and Kate had only survived the wreckage of the early parts of their marriage by going through some seriously difficult things.

Had she truly thought that love was only lovely evening embraces and romantic silhouettes? Had she believed that there wouldn't be hard nights, deep pain, and a need to forgive and to be forgiven?

She hadn't, but she'd certainly been living like she had.

The slider door behind her swished open and then shut into the quiet of this still night. Brayden's footfalls behind her were soft and stopped a bit short of her back. For several breaths, he remained unmoving behind her. Then, "It's a pretty view."

"It is." She glanced back at him, hoping he saw openness in her expression.

One step and he closed the gap between them and stood at her side. He pressed his palms on the rail. "Thank you for coming with me."

When he'd asked her to come with him, he seemed afraid she'd say no. That she'd tell him she'd rather go back home to her parents again. Honestly, a great part of her had wanted to.

The wall remained between them.

And will remain until you fully forgive.

Nerves twisted in her gut, spiraling through her body as she reached to cover Brayden's hand. She heard his quick inhale, felt him hold his breath, and then slowly, as if moving to touch a wounded puppy, he turned his hand until his palm met hers. Audrey looked up, and their gazes met. His thumb brushed over her fingers.

As silence drifted between them, the longing in her heart that had been sparked moments before grew. Audrey turned her face and settled her gaze back on the dock below.

"I'm heartbroken for them," she whispered. "And yet I'm jealous of them." She looked up at her husband again, wondering if he'd understand her absurd claim.

Brayden lifted her hand and tucked it close to his heart. "You want what they have."

She nodded, flattening her palm against his chest. The rhythm that beat beneath her fingers throbbed strong.

He rubbed her shoulder, and when she didn't stiffen, lifted his hand to cradle her face. "Me too."

The places that had remained hard and cold and lifeless in her heart softened, and Audrey held a steady look on him, knowing that he'd read the longing in her eyes.

His head lowered and pressed against hers, and the kick of his heart beneath her touch raced. "I want that with you."

Audrey slid her hand up his chest and collar until she cupped his neck. His exhale was long and slow, warm breath feathering her cheek and then her neck as he moved to pull her in close.

"Please forgive me." His deep plea spilled into her ear from lips that brushed her skin. "I want to be the man you thought I would be. To my dying breath, I'm going to work at it, I promise. Please tell me that, even after all we've been through, you can still love me."

A lump swelled hot in her throat. She swallowed against it and made herself speak. "I forgive you." The wall trembled.

His arms around her tightened.

"I forgive you," she said again, this time with more conviction. Bricks toppled.

The shoulders beneath her hands trembled.

"I still love you." She leaned back. Framed his head with her hands and waited for those sad brown eyes to meet hers. The barrier continued to give way. "I still love you, Brayden, and I want a life with you."

"Audrey . . ." The brokenness in his wavering voice pierced her heart.

There was more she needed to say if she truly wanted healing between them. With a long pull of air that smelled wonderfully like him, she pushed forward. "I need you to forgive me too."

His brow knit, and he shook his head.

"I do, and I need to say this. For both of us. You led, and I followed. Because I wanted to. I wanted you. It didn't matter the cost. It didn't matter that the people closest to us warned us that we were making mistakes. I wanted what I wanted, no different than you. This is our mess, yours and mine."

Lips rolled tight together, Brayden looked like he wanted to argue with her. But instead he nodded. "Our mess. But it doesn't have to stay that way." Though hesitant, he dared to dip his mouth to hers, brushing her lips with the faintest kiss.

"No," she whispered. Her fingers slid into his hair, and she nudged his head back down to hers. This time, she was the one to taste his mouth. "No, we don't have to stay that way."

"Audrey." He kissed her again. "Wife." And again. "I love you."

She whispered his name, and he paused to search her eyes. "I love you," she said.

Brayden found her mouth again, and as passion swept them up together, this time, perhaps for the first time, it felt pure.

Epilogue

(IN WHICH LOVE REMAINS AFTER ALL)

He waited until she stood apart from the many well-wishers—and there were so many of those. His massive family, with all the brothers, the sisters-in-law and nine growing nieces and nephews, not to mention his delighted parents. Her smaller but no less joyous family, including the Alexanders, who would forever be precious to her heart. Such an outpouring of love and excitement for an occasion that could have been marked quietly, perhaps even shamefully, had not grace intervened.

He'd been right, back when he'd told her that sometimes disappointment was a gift. A protection, and a path to something so much better than what had been hoped. Every day since that chilly November evening, he'd wondered on that truth. Hopefully, he'd have it at hand the next time God took away something he thought he should have. God was always good, even in lives that struggled with surrender, with dark valleys, and with ways that were not always fun.

God was good.

And true love was pure.

That was the reason he sought her when she was at the tree line alone. Her eyes brightened in warm greeting as he approached, that soft, lovely smile of hers melting his heart. Reaching for her hand as he closed the space, Brayden returned that tender grin. "Taking a breather?"

"Just for a minute." She scanned the yard boasting the party held especially for them. "Megan always was a little over the top."

Brayden chuckled. "She and Brandon are such opposites."

"Yes. And they're wonderful together."

Squeezing her fingers, he brought them to his lips. "They are that. But they're not why I came over here to you."

"No?"

He winked. "I have something for you, for this first anniversary we almost didn't reach."

At that, a mild frown pressed her lovely mouth. "We made it," she said, as if she felt he needed to remember that.

"We did. However . . ." He began working the ring he'd placed on her left hand the day she'd graduated, twisting gently and moving it up her finger. "I don't want you to wear this anymore."

Snatching her hand back, Audrey breathed a little gasp. "What?"

With gentle persistence, he reclaimed her hand. "Audrey, this stone"—he finished removing her ring—"is fake." He paused, holding his look on her to gauge her reaction.

A small scowl folded her brow, but then she cleared it away, lifting her chin. "I don't care. It's just a rock."

"That may be true, but I do care." With the hand that wasn't holding that fake diamond, he fished in his dress pants pocket and pulled out a small band. The stone set in this white gold was half the size of the cubic zirconia, but it had cost him ten times as much. All that he could afford.

He repositioned her hand and slid the new ring in place. "It's not as big, not as showy." Ring in place, he folded her hand against his chest and sought those green eyes. "But it's real."

Audrey blinked as she looked up at him, and then she stepped nearer and slid her free palm to cradle his face. "I love it," she whispered. "Thank you."

Leaning down to meet her upturned mouth, Brayden kissed his wife tenderly. After a breathless, beautiful moment, Audrey pulled away. With a loving smile, she sighed and then turned to face the yard full of people who had come to celebrate their year-old marriage.

Standing at her back, Brayden wrapped his arms around her shoulders and savored the pure joy of her leaning against his chest. A move of trust, of security. Something that six months past, he had barely hoped for from her. Had it only been six months? So much had changed. In his heart, and between them.

Taking one of his hands, Audrey gently repositioned his arm and pressed his palm to her belly. A thrill spiraled through him. November, she'd said. This little one, who was still hidden in the precious folds of the pure love that had grown between them, already lived in his heart. He'd been praying over this gift of life ever since Audrey had whispered her news, as he did so in that moment.

Evidence of grace, as was this joyous gathering of family and friends celebrating, a year later, Mr. and Mrs. Brayden Murphy. *So* much had changed.

Praise God!

He turned his face and delighted in the warm smell of her. Nuzzling her lovely strawberry-blond hair, though he preferred it curly to this straight business she'd worked it into earlier that morning, he pressed a kiss near her ear. "You are lovely, my wife," he whispered.

The lift of a small smile moved her cheeks.

He kissed her jaw. "Do you know you have my heart?"

"All of it?" she teased. The very fact that she would say such a thing with lightness was more proof of so much.

"Every inch, my love."

Audrey hummed a contented sigh.

"Do I have yours?" He was not above such fishing. Pride had been dismantled, and hallelujah for it. It'd done him little good and much harm. Nothing had become more important to him than the state of this woman's heart. He wanted it whole and happy, and he wanted to possess hers as she did his.

Audrey tilted her chin so her green eyes found his. Soft and adoring, shimmering in the twinkling glitter of the café lights strung throughout the Alexanders' backyard, her gaze warmed him clean through. "Forever."

Further proof of so much.

These moments were miracles. Signs of grace and mercy rained down by One who could redeem. One who could transform, whether Brayden deserved it or not. He didn't, and he was well aware of that reality. But he continued to ask for God's transformation in his life, that He would mold him into a better man.

Why God had seen fit to do so much for one such as Brayden, he could not comprehend. But neither could he deny it—nor would he ever want to. Instead, he'd focus on lifting such glorious gifts up in grateful praise.

Because after all, there was this. There was love.

The End

Whew!

That one was a bit rough, wasn't it? Thank you for persevering with me. Would you mind leaving a review for other readers, sharing your honest thoughts about After All? Thank you!

I'm guessing you have a few questions you'd like answered . . . such as what's going to happen with Sadie and Connor, yes? There's bad news, and there's good news. I'll give you the good news: there's another Murphy Brothers Story ready for you. Morning by Morning is perhaps the most emotional tales of the group, but I've been told it's worth the tough journey. I hope you'll go along with me on it.

As always, my friend, I thank you for joining me on this journey through family, faith, and love.

Printed in Great Britain
by Amazon